James L. Bowen

The Doomed Hunter

Or, the tragedy of Forest Valley: a story of the early West

James L. Bowen

The Doomed Hunter
Or, the tragedy of Forest Valley: a story of the early West

ISBN/EAN: 9783337393892

Printed in Europe, USA, Canada, Australia, Japan

Cover: Foto ©Andreas Hilbeck / pixelio.de

More available books at **www.hansebooks.com**

THE

DOOMED HUNTER;

OR,

THE TRAGEDY OF FOREST VALLEY.

A STORY OF THE EARLY WEST.

By JAMES L. BOWEN,

AUTHOR OF " FRONTIER SCOUTS," " SCOUTING DAVE," ETC.

LONDON :
GEORGE ROUTLEDGE & SONS,
THE BROADWAY, LUDGATE.

THE DOOMED HUNTER.

CHAPTER I

THE FUR DEALER AND THE HUNTER.

IT is no extraordinary circumstance in the history of our Western civilization that a howling wilderness—the abode only of wild animals and wilder savages—becomes transformed, in a few years, to a smiling agricultural district, with populous towns and villages. The broad, fertile fields, rich in their harvest wealth, present little to mark the scene over which white men and savages fought in relentless warfare during the incipience of those settlements. Occasionally it may be said of a certain locality that a pitched battle ·occurred in that spot, or some noted personage was slain thereabouts. But, the strategy, the struggles, the daring which wrested those lands from the sullen Indian, and held them against the wiles of his power, those are passed over and forgotten.

The railroad which to-day passes through the thriving town of C—, in Ohio, crosses a small creek some little distance before reaching the village. Leaving the railroad at this point, and dropping every modern association of the place, let us go back to the time of the first settlers. It is not very many years—precisely how many is no matter of especial interest. Suffice it is to say that at that time the primeval forests still lined the banks of Silver Run, as the little stream had been named by the first settlers.

Then, as now, its waters ran in crystal pureness, murmuring lovingly as they hastened on to join the larger stream, and in turn to be emptied into the, broad Ohio. Native verdure in rich luxuriance lined the watercourse, and animal and insect life abounded in profusion.

Here a gallant body of pioneers had halted, struck by the beauty of the scenery, the abundance of game, and an unusually good water-privilege, which could be employed for the various purposes requiring "power." Selecting a rich bottom, they built a settlement, surrounded by hills upon nearly every side.

The site had been named "Forest Valley," and certainly no appellation could have been more characteristic and appropriate.

Several years had passed, during which the settlement grew and throve. At the time when our story opens it contained nearly twenty dwellings, a rude church, with blacksmith-shop and store.

The latter was such an institution as the needs of the community demanded—where furs and the few productions of the forest-homes found a ready exchange for powder and lead, bad whisky and Indian trinkets, besides such articles as were needed by the settlers in their more peaceful pursuits.

The store, and, indeed, the majority of the buildings in Forest Valley, belonged to a person named Jehonikam Andrews—a man who had noticed the fine points of the settlement, and at once invested his all in such ways as nearly to monopolize the active power of the place. Notwithstanding the facts that his prices were enormous, and that various stories circulated in regard to his weights and measures, there was no course left to the settlers but to patronize him.

The mill had been built by his capital, and the lumber which it had turned into his hands had been employed in the erection of new houses, all of which found ready occupants, even if Jehonikam's prices and terms were slightly outrageous.

Apart from his love of money and position, he was not considered a bad citizen, and many little acts of kindness showed that good lurked beneath an almost miserly exterior. Indeed, with those who were independent of him, Jehonikam was chatty and sociable, disposed to laugh and joke with a hearty relish. But all familiarity from those who were in his power was nipped in the bud.

The habitation in which Andrews dwelt was a small house situated near the "store." His family consisted merely of a pleasant, beautiful daughter, twenty years of age, Nancy Andrews by name, and himself. His day was spent in the store and around the place, excepting only service hours on Sunday, when he was foremost in the little church, where a simple-minded divine dealt out stereotyped truths from Sunday to Sunday.

As Jehonikam only ate and slept at home, it is but natural that we should find him in the store the moment we introduce the opening scene of our story. A counter ran from one side of the apartment to the other, a rude writing-desk rising at one extremity, at which Jehonikam was busy with a greasy account-book. But two others were in the store at the time, one of whom immediately took his leave, with a small bundle, the proceeds of his barter with the merchant.

The other was a tall and muscular young man, clad in the ordinary garb of a hunter. He was leaning against the counter, his dark eyes bent upon the floor in a deep study. Occasionally he glanced up at the merchant, who

8 THE DOOMED HUNTER.

remained for some minutes busy with his accounts, then turned his gaze again upon the floor.

After he had waited for some time, Jehonikam closed his book, rolled up the furs for which he had just made a shrewd bargain, and tossed them into a drawer, which he carefully locked. Having nothing else to occupy his attention, he now turned to the man who had been awaiting his somewhat tardy movements.

"Wal, Ralph," he said, in tones which sounded almost harsh, "you said you wanted to consult with me a little. I don't know's I've anything on hand jest at this particular minute. So if you'll say right off what's wanting, I'll try and see what can be done for ye."

"True, I asked for your private ear a minute," the other said, hesitatingly. "I have come to you upon a matter such as I never spoke of before. I don't know but you'll think I'm rather bold to ask you for such a great favour."

Ralph Rilley paused, evidently at a loss how to proceed, which Jehonikam perceived, and came to his rescue promptly.

"Never mind, Ralph," he said. "If you want any advance on your next lot o' fur, or anything out o' the store, don't be afeard to speak right up. I know you too well to be afeared to trust ye."

"No, sir; that is not it," was the quick reply. "I have yet some money, though I paid you quite a sum, for me, a few days since. But I have my house and farm— that is to be—paid for now, and I have been thinking that I might as well conclude to marry and settle down for life!"

The last words were spoken somewhat hesitatingly, and the earnest eyes of the speaker sought the floor again while a deep blush suffused his handsome face. But the unpleasant sensation quickly passed away, and he looked the shrewd fur-dealer respectfully in the face, as the latter returned :—

"By all means. I was married afore I was as old as you are this blessed minute! I don't believe in any, man's waitin' till the last crack of doomsday! If you want to git married and take comfort, why dew it; that's my style. And if there's anything I can do to help the matter along, jest name it, and I will lend you a hand."

"Thank you, sir, for the kindness. I have found the woman to make me happy through life, and if you will but give your consent to our marriage, all will be very near to completion."

"Wal, why don't ye say on?" demanded Jehonikam, who evidently suspected what was coming, as the young man stopped, and his eyes again sought the floor. "What is your purpose in coming to me about it at all?"

"The lady whom I love is your daughter, sir. I have come to ask your consent to our marriage!"

"What is that I hear?" demanded the enraged parent. "Do you dare come to me with such a proposal?"

"I dare nothing of the kind, sir," replied Ralph, from whom all signs of fear and trembling had now departed. "I merely came to present our mutual wishes, and ask your sanction!"

"Your mutual wishes, indeed! I should like to have you tell me the meaning of that word. You don't suppose for one minute that my Nancy would think of marrying such a wild man as yourself?"

"I feared such would be the case," returned Ralph. "But as she sent me to you, after saying she loved me, and was willing to become my wife—"

"Bosh! bosh!" interrupted Jehonikam, assuming a confidential tone. "The girl was only making gammon of you, Ralph. She has a lover in the East, one that will make her a worthy husband, and she knows it. She never would have said any such thing, unless in mere sport. So I advise you to go quickly home, and say no more about anything so foolish!"

"I tell you 'tis nothing foolish, Mr. Andrews. I love her, and she loves me. I know that. I will endeavour to make her happy, and—"

"You will do nothing of the kind!" exclaimed Andrews, passionately. "I tell you she is not for you, or such as you; so let that be enough."

"Haven't I always conducted myself honourably in any transactions with you?" Ralph demanded, stung by the tone and bearing of his interlocutor.

"Because you couldn't do anything else," growlingly returned Jehonikam.

"Haven't I always conducted myself honourably with all who have had anything to do with me? Did you ever hear anything spoken against me by those who know me best?"

The speaker fixed an eagle glance upon Andrews, and the latter quailed before it. He knew that the young man was honoured by all who knew him, and his own experience had been sufficient to satisfy him that Ralph would make his mark in the world. Yet, the "almighty dollar" stood before his vision, and he never could think of such a thing as bestowing his daughter upon a comparatively poor young man, while there was any chance of her becoming the bride of one more blessed in worldly possessions. Without raising his eyes to Rilley's face, he said :—

" What is the use of all this? What has your character to do with me or mine ? "

" Just this," was the firm reply. " I love your daughter, and my determination is to marry her—come what will. The only objection you could raise is that of character, and since I am all right in that respect, I fancy that Nancy will have a will of her own in the matter."

" Beware, sir !" thundered the fur-dealer, as he bent a fierce scowl upon the young man. " Do not dare to insult me in my own house ! "

" I do not dare anything," returned the other, calmly. " I had anticipated your answer, and we consulted together in the matter before I came here. Nancy assured me that she would accept me as a husband, and I shall not withdraw, certainly."

Jehonikam vaulted over the counter, and pointed to the door. His face was flushed with passion, and it seemed with difficulty that he refrained from laying violent hands upon Ralph.

" Go !" he exclaimed. " Never dare to set yourself over the door-sill again until you have made due apologies for your indecent conduct. Go, I say ! Don't you hear ?"

" Certainly, sir. And since the house is yours I have no intention but to obey. Still, I can assure you that the day is not very far distant when you will repent of all this."

The words reached the ears of several persons passing at the time, as also the angry rejoinder of Jehonikam :—

" Never come into this store again, you presuming puppy ; if you do, I'll thrash you out of it ! "

Ralph had little fear of the threat being carried out, but he did not wish a quarrel with the purse-proud fur-

dealer, and drew himself away from the vicinity, regardless of the numerous questions pressed upon him by those
who had overheard the storekeeper's words.

Having settled his perturbed spirits into something of
order, Ralph turned upon his heel, and made a straight
cut to the house where the object of his affections resided.
Of course, he was met at the door by Nancy in person, and
they were soon seated in the house, discussing the answer
given by Jehonikam.

The fur-dealer happened to take a fancy similar to that
of Ralph.

"Likely enough he'll be up to the house, fust I'll know,"
he muttered. "I'll just slip up and let that gal know
that he ain't to cross the threshold on any condition. She
needn't think to fall in love with every boy that comes
along; she hain't head to choose for her own welfare yet.
I must talk with her on the subject when I get time."

Thus meditating he closed and locked the principal
door to the store, and slipping out by a back way, started
directly toward the house. He arrived soon after Ralph
and Nancy had taken a seat, and entered the room before
either of them noticed his presence. Nancy uttered a cry
as she beheld his angry and threatening looks.

"So I find you in my own house, viper, !" exclaimed
Jehonikam, brandishing a cane as the youth rose to his
feet. "I'll teach you to defy me in this way !"

And flourishing the walking-stick he sprung in the
direction of Ralph, intending to give him a sound
thrashing.

"No, no, father," pleaded Nancy, as she stepped
before him ; "you must not hurt Ralph !"

But the angry father pushed her rudely aside, and the
next moment found himself locked in the embrace of

Ralph. The young hunter was muscular, extremely so, and though Jehonikam was nearly his equal in bulk, he was far from possessing his strength. In vain he attempted to use his staff. It was wrenched from his hand, and himself raised bodily in the arms of the man he would have chastised, and carried to his own door.

Nor did the young man stop there. Directly into the street he proceeded with his burden, and upon setting him down, Ralph remarked :—

"Now, sir, we are upon ground where each has an equal right, and if you attempt to disturb me, I shall forget everything else, and defend myself to the utmost. I warn you that you will get no tender treatment, after what has passed !"

Thus speaking Ralph placed his unwilling burden upon his feet, and released his hold. For a moment it seemed the baffled fur-dealer could not restrain his wrath, but after gazing upon the athletic form of the man before him, he swallowed it, saying :—

"I only want you never to darken a door of mine again."

"If I do you will be very likely to know it," was all the answer the young man vouchsafed ; and as a crowd was collecting, Jehonikam beat a retreat toward his store.

As before, the bystanders eagerly demanded to know the cause of the tumult. But Ralph would not gratify them, and the fur-dealer was too deeply wrought upon to submit to any questioning.

CHAPTER II.

THE TRAGEDY.

Two days had passed since the little event recorded in the preceding chapter. Night and darkness reigned over Forest Valley. Suddenly a wild, sharp cry—that cry which ever conveys such terror in settlements like that in question—rang out upon the midnight air :—

" Fire ! Fire ! !"

One sturdy pair of lungs after another took up the shout, and the startled sleepers rushed forth from their homes to combat the dreaded enemy.

Ralph Rilley lay upon his couch, not sleeping, but gazing and thinking. The first alarm reached his ear, and without pausing he sprung out, hastily dressed, and was soon in the open air.

At first he saw no indications of any fire, but joining the hurrying crowd he soon found that the flames were kindled, or had broken out, within the little dwelling occupied by Jehonikam Andrews. Though their progress was as yet confined to one room, it seemed questionable whether the building could be saved.

A fire was far from being an everyday occurrence, and the first efforts of the startled inhabitants were far from being in the right direction. Confused running about and shouting seemed to be the extent of active measures for subduing the threatened conflagration.

With a quicker eye and clearer brain than others, Ralph saw the state of affairs. Selecting such men as had buckets, he formed a line from the bank of the creek to the dwelling, and as buckets of water were passed rapidly along, he dashed them in person upon the flames.

Shouts of applause went up as the progress of the

flames was checked, and those who had laboured thus far were relieved by others from the crowd. Renewed exertions brought corresponding success, and in a short time the glad tidings went from one anxious lip to another,

" The fire is out ! "

Withdrawing, then, from his post of honour, Ralph ran his eye rapidly over the faces of those assembled. But the features he sought were not there.

" Where are the people of the house ?" he demanded.

Sure enough—where were they ? None had seen either Jehonikam or his daughter since the outburst of the fire. During the fearful excitement which prevailed, no one had thought of it. But now an immediate search was instituted.

After calling aloud until satisfied that they were not in the vicinity, lights were procured, and a party set about exploring the house. The room where the fire had occurred was perfectly bare, and they immediately pushed on to the next.

As the door of the latter was opened a horrid sight met their gaze. Lying upon the floor, in a pool of his own blood, was Jehonikam Andrews ! The room being filled with smoke, he was lifted and borne to the open air, where a hasty examination was held.

It was evident from the first that he was dead. An examination of the body showed several deep cuts, one upon the back plainly indicating that he could not have given the fatal blow himself. Besides he had been stabbed through the heart, which was evidently the immediate cause of his death.

The anger and excitement which prevailed as these developments were reached baffle description. The com-

motion when the fire raged most fully was nothing in
comparison. Strong men raved and wept by turns,
vowing deadly vengeance upon the cowardly murderer;
while women and children gathered in weeping masses,
and strove to reassure each other, each more frightened
than her neighbour.

All, save Ralph, were thoroughly overcome by the
fearful revelations. He merely satisfied himself that
Jehonikam was past all human assistance, and then he
started in search of Nancy. If harm had befallen the
father, what more likely than that the daughter was also
involved! The very thought was fearful to the bold
hunter.

Hastily summoning one or two assistants, who grasped
lights, they turned away and completed the exploration of
the house. Indeed, only the chamber remained to be
searched. It was reached by a rough stairway, which
had been partially burned down, so that it required a deal
of care to ascend. But Ralph heeded not the peril. With
a few quick bounds he reached the floor above, and his
companions could do no less than to follow his impulsive
lead.

But when the chamber was reached, and the light had
brought all its outlines into view, a low cry of distress
broke from the hunter's lips. The one he sought was not
there!

The bed upon which she had been sleeping was there,
and its appearance indicated that she had passed several
hours in slumber. But she was gone! None of her
clothing remained, so it was evident that her departure
had been expected, or that she had been allowed time to
select necessary articles of apparel.

A quick search convinced Ralph that her body was not

within the confines of the building, and then he hastened back to the excited group about the body of Jehonikam with the painful intelligence. Of course, the former commotion was increased rather than allayed by this additional evil.

To render assurance doubly sure, messengers were despatched to every house, to make certain that she had not fled there in a moment of terror. These soon returned with tidings that she was not in the place, neither had any person seen her since the previous evening. The nearest dwellers, who resided at some little distance, had heard no confusion, and only a person in the lower portion of the village, who was watching with a sick child, had discovered the fire in time to prevent a general conflagration.

The mystery which surrounded all the facts of the case, served to make the citizens more eager for the solving of the problem. Nothing of the kind had been known to them before, and common safety demanded that such an example be made as should thoroughly intimidate all lawless characters in the future.

Actuated by these feelings and motives, Ralph, who was certainly the hero of the night, took a blazing torch, and suggested that the room in which the body had been found be thoroughly examined, since something might be found from which proof could be obtained.

Strangely enough, this had been neglected thus far, but the idea was a good one, and immediately acted upon. Three men besides Ralph were selected to make a careful inspection of the apartment. Being well provided with lights they entered the house, and closed the door, that no intruders might disturb them in the operation.

There were evidences of a severe though short struggle

having taken place. The only chair in the room had been overturned and broken, and the bed much disarranged—evidently after the occupant had risen.

The clothes which Jehonikam had laid aside on retireing for the night still were lying in a corner, trampled in a confused mass. One of the men, named Alfred Adams, raised them in his hand, and was proceeding to search them for any indications of robbery, when something fell to the floor.

" Here is the tool with which the cursed deed was performed," said Adams, raising a long bloody knife, and holding it up to the view of the others. " This will give us a clue."

" Seems to me I've see'd that 'ere knife afore," remarked William Rufus, casting a sly glance at Ralph.

The latter drew near, and as his eyes rested upon the knife, he gave a surprised exclamation.

" That is mine !" he said, frankly.

The astonishment of those with him was certainly intense. They drew near, and for a few moments gazed from the knife to its owner in mute wonder. The weapon was an ordinary hunting-knife, with buck-horn handle, upon the upper end of which were engraved the letters " R. R."

" Sartin it's yourn," said Rufus, with a slight bow. " I reckin thar's anuff in this place knows that knife, so't ye needn't try to deny it."

" I had no intention of denying it," returned Ralph, almost sharply. " Did I not tell you that it was my knife ?"

" Then how came it here ?" was the quick demand of the others within the apartment.

" I am sure I cannot say," was the earnest reply.

"It must have been stolen from my room by the murderer, if it was used in that foul deed."

"Oh, sartin! We all believe that!" said Rufus, somewhat spitefully. "None of us remember the fight you had with Mister Andrews two or three days ago!"

There was something so impertinently malicious in the tone of the speaker, that Ralph started as if stung by a viper.

"You do not mean to insinuate that I am guilty of this dreadful crime?" he demanded, his soul shrinking in terror from the very thought.

"I didn't say nothin' about it," was returned, with a grin of triumph, "but if ye want my opinion, I must say that it looks pretty dark for ye."

"And you?" the young man asked, casting a glance around upon the others. "You certainly cannot think me guilty of such a dreadful crime."

"I hate to think it, Ralph," said Adams, who still held the knife; " but, as Rufus says, it certainly looks quite dark against you. Everybody knows of your quarrel with Jehonikam, and I have heard much wonderment as to the cause. This, with the finding of your knife in this dreadful state, will tell hard against you, unless something else should transpire. You see what a phase these facts put upon the case."

"Yes; I see," returned Ralph, who hardly yet understood the true light in which he was placed; "but, I declare, and swear, with all heaven to witness, that I know no more of the manner in which that knife came here than yourself. I had not touched it for two weeks, and supposed it lying in my room at my brother's house."

"Hadn't you better try to prove that you and Andrews was on the best of terms?" Rufus insinuated.

" I've knowed the poor man for a number o' years, and you's the first one I ever knowed turned out'n his house. I thort 'twan't all right when I see'd ye so desput a-tryin' to put out the fire. They dew say 'straws show which way the wind blows' sometimes."

The search was continued for some time longer, the closest scrutiny being given to every article, and no crack or crevice escaping the general inspection. But search as they would—and none could be more anxious than Ralph, since his very life depended upon the fruits of it —nothing transpired. Beyond the finding of the knife, there was not the slightest trace to be gained of the perpetrators.

With sorrowful faces the party unclosed the door, and prepared to step forth. A crowd without was clamorous to learn the result of their investigations.

" You will pardon us for detaining you," said Alfred Adams, gently, as he took Ralph by the arm. " I really trust that you are not guilty ; but, you know, we have settled here in the wilderness, and, being under the control of no responsible legal power, we have sworn to support strict justice among ourselves, man for man."

" I know," said Ralph, with a swelling breast, "you have the right to detain me as a prisoner, and I cannot resist. I only swear to you that I am innocent, and I trust to prove that innocence fully."

" Hope you will—hope you will ! " was the really kind reply.

Then holding the bloody knife in his hand, Adams made his way toward the body of Andrews. His grasp rested upon one arm of Ralph, and a companion held the other. Rufus, who had an intolerant prejudice against the prisoner, though without any cause, had dived into the crowd, and was busily engaged in spreading the story of Ralph's guilt.

Adams, upon his part, made a clear and careful statement of the circumstances under which the knife had been found, and examination revealed beyond the shadow of a doubt that the wounds had been given with the identical instrument.

Here the controversy ended, since nothing further could be proved. The young hunter reiterated his innocence, and declared again that he knew nothing of the affair, and had no knowledge that the knife which did the fatal deed was out of his room at his brother's house.

But, in the excited state of the community, they did not pause to reason. Various stories which had been covertly circulated since the somewhat open rupture between the prisoner and deceased were repeated. The threat which several testified to having heard used so recently also weighed against him, and in a short time more than three-fourths of those present had expressed their conviction that Ralph was guilty.

Suddenly the loud voice of William Rufus broke out :—

" See here, men," he said, mounting a block of wood that he might be more conspicuous, " we all know that feller's the guilty one. You know what we said when the thing was first done—how we'd punish anybody that had cut up so ; now, don't le's be respecters of persons. Thar's plenty of trees hyarabouts—why don't we string him up? We know he's the one ! "

" Yes—string him up ! String him up ! " responded various voices in chorus. " We'll set an example, if it does come a little tough at fust ! "

The proposition instantly gained ground, and hanging was not the only means suggested.

"Burn him!"   "Shoot him!"   "Chop his head off!
"Roast him!" were some of the modes suggested by the
rough crowd, as being more satisfactory than simple
hanging.

Ralph began to tremble, as well he might, at the
rapidly-increasing violence of the exasperated settlers.
Death, speedy and awful, stared him in the face! He
attempted to expostulate with the multitude, but in vain.
His friends, few in number, also joined in the protest, but
all was of no avail.

The tumult increased momentarily. Torches were
brought in abundance, ropes produced, and clamorous
cries for the prisoner's death resounded more and more
fiercely.

It was a fearful scene, as revealed by that uncertain
torchlight.   The stark, cold body of the murdered man;
the pale and anxious prisoner; the agitated and surging
mass of angry men, with pale, distressed, and weeping
women and children in the background, lighted by the
ghastly and flickering torches.

Suddenly a fresh cry was raised, and, headed by the
zealous William Rufus, the avengers of blood dashed
toward the young hunter.

CHAPTER III.

THE DOOMED HUNTER.

"Come, sir," said the over-zealous leader of the mob,
"we are sorry to put ye to any trouble; but it won't dew
to let ye go loose any longer. Some of ye jest tie the
feller's hands ahind his back, so he won't be dangerous,
and we'll hev' a show here what never was see'd afore in
Forset Valley, not by a long run."

Several men seized the hunter's arms, and forced them behind him, where they were very speedily tied. Then, that their momentary frenzy might not abate, and that good counsels might not prevail, he was dragged from the place, out into the margin of the forest, something like forty rods from the scene of excitement.

Of course, his few friends followed, anxious to take any advantage which might present itself. Even a few of the women and children were drawn to the spot by an uncontrollable desire to witness the strange and deadly proceedings.

"Here's a good place," Rufus exclaimed, as he came to a stop. His assistants gathered around, and declared that it could not be bettered.

They were beneath a huge oak, which threw out a heavy lateral branch, at the height of ten or twelve feet. Nature evidently had saved the infatuated men the trouble of erecting a gallows.

"Thar' can't be nothin' better," observed one or two, after a hasty glance around them. "Swing the murderer up; don't wait for any parley! It's the only way where there's no law."

"Tie his legs fust," commanded the leader. "We don't want him makin' tew much of a figure arter we've got him swung over our heads."

The command was obeyed, a strong rope being bound about the prisoner's ankles in the securest manner possible.

"Better tie a stone, or a good sized stick of wood, to his feet, so't his neck won't prove too strong for his body," suggested a third speaker.

"No use of it," declared Rufus. "I know suthin' how heavy he is, and thar's no danger but his neck'll give way in good time. Just put on the rope and swing him up over that limb, and I'll warrant ye he never'll stab another man in the back!"

A sharp hiss ran through the crowd at this allusion to the most disgusting feature of the whole affair, and fresh cries were raised, "String him up!"

"I could go anything else," said Rufus, when quiet was partially restored, "but the idea of being stabbed in the back always makes me feel bad myself. But it ain't too late now. If you say, Let him off, or, Wait a few days, we kin dew that."

One or two of the young man's friends ventured to suggest leniency, but their voices were drowned in the tumult raised by those who were anxious for what they deemed to be summary justice. Even threats of personal violence were not wanting toward those advocating mercy to Ralph.

This Rufus had foreseen, and his words were expressly calculated to inflame his hearers. Seeing that their feelings were brought to a pitch where all reason was set at defiance, he slightly changed his tone, professing reluctance to take any further part in the execution.

"I'm sure every scoundrel ought to have his pay for what evil deeds he cuts up; but for my part I can't bear the idea of hangin' a man any way. If you insist on that, some of you will have it to do."

"Then out o' the way!" growled a gruff fellow, who had been impatiently swinging the end of a rope in which he had made a noose. "If you darn't swing the feller up, hyar's one what ain't afeared."

With a satanic leer he threw the rope over the limb above, and brought the noose down to a convenient height.

"Jest bring on the feller!" he shouted   "We'll soon

show him a new mode of dancin'; let him dance on nothin' awhile."

The pale victim was led forward. A group of the latter's friends had gathered at a little distance, and for a moment they even contemplated force in attempting to defeat the purposed execution. But they readily saw that all such efforts on their part must be in vain. They were outnumbered, more than four to one, and they had no positive grounds upon which to claim the doomed one's innocence. Determined not to witness the last fearful struggle, they turned away toward the settlement.

Ralph was led beneath the fatal noose, and the rope adjusted to his neck. Thus far he may have entertained hopes that his doom would be averted, or at least postponed. But now all hope was ended. He felt the rough cord passed around his neck, and drawn to an uncomfortable tightness. He attempted to speak, for he wished to repeat his entire innocence, but an angry clamour drowned his words, and a broad palm was placed over his mouth. Since he could not speak to his fellow-men, the doomed one turned his thoughts heavenward, and breathed a silent prayer for strength to bear the last trying ordeal.

Here his silent supplications ceased, for four strong men grasped the rope, and at a word from their leader the young hunter's body was swung into the air. A few even ventured to applaud the terrible spectacle, but the majority looked on in silent awe at the work of death before them.

For a short time the sense of pain and strangulation was fearful, but that gradually passed away, and only a wide blank, devoid of life and sensation, seemed to spread before the suffering young man.

Suddenly a yell—wild, loud, long, and fierce—broke

from the forest near them. The party about the oak started fearfully at this indication of others' presence, and endeavoured to pierce the gloomy forest shades. Even while they gazed and wondered, a burst of flame broke from the neighbouring covert, a few balls and many arrows hurtled through the air and fell in the midst of the frightened group.

" Indians ! Indians !" burst from more than one ashy lip, and several of their number fell before the deadly volley, killed or wounded.

Of course, the advantage was all with the assailants. The whites were brought out full by the strong torchlight around them, and their foes were in the deepest shade. Besides, scarcely a man in the group was armed, none having deemed weapons necessary for their enterprise, or having thought of them at all in the terrible commotion of that night.

As the arrows continued to fly about them, the party broke and ran, regardless of the suspended Ralph, who came to the ground with a thump.

No sooner did the settlers show their backs than the Indians gave another yell, and charged upon the rear-most of the flying horde. Frantic with terror, the men rushed in every direction, and not till they were dispersed beyond all possibility of recall, for some time at least, did the savages give over the pursuit.

Then, at a signal, they rallied, and returned to the fatal oak. Those who had fallen and remained there, whether dead or wounded, were tomahawked and scalped without mercy, after which the Indians attended to the fallen Ralph.

That individual had no full realization of his state, or of the bloody drama enacting around him. The shout, and firing, and his own fall had been like portions of a confused nightmare to him. Whether they were souuds from this world or the other, he knew not.

At length he begau slowly to regain consciousness. The rope still held his throat in a suffocating grasp, but it was gradually relaxing, and he was able to breathe with some difficulty. His first realizations were of a comfortable feeling of freedom, after which his faculties returned quite rapidly.

The first defined seusation which he had, was that some persons were about him, and the impression which he experienced most naturally was that he had been let down before life was extinct, either through mistake or because his executioners had relented. But he soon comprehended that something unusual had taken place. All was dark around, in the absence of the glaring torchlight which had last greeted his eyes. Numerous persons were moving around, and they occasionally spoke in muffled tones, but he could understand nothing of what was said.

Suddenly the truth burst upon him. An Indian assault had been made, aud he was now in the power of the savages. What did that fact presage? He knew very well that the red men were far from being merciful, and though he had occasionally heard of persons being made prisoners by them, it was the exception, and not the rule.

His conflicting hopes and fears soon were put at rest by the appearance of a tall, athletic Indian, who bent over him, and placed a hand upon his brow. Then he turned toward his companions and gruuted something in gutturals which the young man could not comprehend.

The savages hastened to the spot, and bending over the half-animated form, proceeded to rub and chafe the limbs, much as white men might have done under the same circumstances. Ralph felt the warmth and vigour rapidly returning to his body, and in a short time he was enabled to raise himself to a sitting position. The Indians muttered their satisfaction at this change, and ceased their vigorous efforts.

Ralph wondered why he was spared. By the very uncertain light he could see that several of the savages carried scalps at their belts, and he expected each moment that his own would be required. But, singularly enough, he was treated with kindness, the party only delaying its departure on his account.

Could it be that they intended taking him along as prisoner? and if so, why? He had never given the Indians cause of offence, to be sure; neither had those who were lying about him in the terrible postures in which they had been overtaken by death. Then a suspicion stole over him. He had been rescued from the jaws of death; might not the Indians calculate upon his turning against the whites, and assisting in their murderous plans? This seemed a natural conclusion, and although his manly soul shrunk from the idea, he resolved to take advantage of the desire, if such it should prove, and preserve his life for the present, even if a temporary sojourn among the Indians were required. He had a double purpose, now, to effect by living—to prove his own innocence of crime, and to find Nancy.

With something of an effort he staggered to his feet, and the same tall Indian whom he had previously observed extended an arm for his support. Though burning with curiosity to know the reason of such apparent friendliness, Ralph forbore to ask any questions, wisely leaving all to the discretion of the savages.

" Pale-face go with Injun ?" the red-man finally grunted out.

" I don't know," returned Ralph. " What shall I go with you for ?"

" Pale-face want to live," sententiously responded the savage. " Him like the young tree with big roots. Him live great while. Make great warrior. But pale-face hang him on a tree. No good fruit for great tree. Make tree die—make hunter die. White man go with Injun. Injun make great man of pale-face, Injun tell pale-face suffin when git to his brothers."

" There's more than a common share of truth in what you say," Ralph replied. " I haven't much fear o' killin' the tree, but I don't want to put it in danger, to say nothing of my own neck. So I conclude it may be best for me to go with you. What is it that you will tell me when we get to your tribe ?"

" You walk ?" demanded the Indian, paying no attention to Ralph's last question.

As the young man knew there would be no heed given to the question, however often repeated, he tried the task of walking, and found that he succeeded much better than might have been expected under the circumstances.

" You walk good," said the Indian, who watched the proceeding closely. " Now we go."

The Indians seemed highly elated at their success, and walked along quite rapidly, apparently paying little heed to the prisoner, who walked among them with all the appearance of a free man. But the covert glances which were cast upon him from time to time, and the impossibility of leaving his place, satisfied him that he was not henceforth to be his own master.

At length they crossed Silver Run, some distance above

Forest Valley, and here he was allowed to drink of the pure waters, and also to bathe his neck and head. This procedure revived him greatly, and gave the wonted elasticity and vigour to his limbs. He was now able to keep pace with the savages without any undue exertion.

It was almost daylight when they crossed Silver Run, and in a few minutes after leaving it the first beams of the morning sun appeared upon the tree-tops. The Indians now hastened their degree of speed, which they could do with safety, and travelled several hours before making any halt.

They then came to a stand near a bountiful spring which gushed from beneath a large rock. Several of the men produced dried meat, which was eagerly devoured by the party, after having been divided. Though Ralph felt little inclination to eat, he took a small piece of the meat, drank from the spring, and then seated himself upon the ground to rest and think, while his captors were satisfying their appetites. He well knew where they were, often having stopped at that spring to quench his thirst when upon hunting excursions. But if that was the most direct course toward the Indian town, he feared that it must be far distant.

Their repast was soon over, and then, resting their wearied frames for a brief time, the march was resumed.

Ralph noticed before leaving the place that one of the number was left behind, and special instructions given him.

CHAPTER IV.

THE INDIAN TOWN.

THE savages pursued a course somewhat to the west of north, and continued to travel at a brisk rate for two or three hours longer. Ralph had counted his swarthy companions, and found their number to be twenty-two present, with their leader, whose Indian name signified Elk's Foot. This, with the one left behind, would make quite a force, nearly man for man, to what the settlers could raise, after the decimation they had recently suffered. The advantage in arms of course lay with the latter, nearly every man possessing a good rifle, and being expert in its use ; while the arms of the Indians consisted in part of firelocks, bows and arrows, and spears, with the never-failing knives and tomahawks for close quarters.

These facts Ralph had noticed, since he felt that the indignant settlers would not allow the matter to rest until they had pursued and if possible wreaked summary vengeance upon the Indians. And while none of his sympathies were with the latter, he hoped certainly that they would escape for the present. He had little doubt that if they were overhauled, and he fell into the hands of the whites, he would meet an instant and ignominious death.

His suspicions of pursuit were soon confirmed. The detonation of a heavily-loaded musket resounded through the forest, and brought every man to a stand-still at once. That they were excited was evident, and yet the natural stoicism of their race was such that its exhibition was suppressed. To the young man's surprise, they remained standing where they were for some minutes—minutes which seemed hours to him.

At length the form of an advancing warrior was seen dashing through the trees, and in a minute he was beside them.

"Pale-faces," he said, pointing back in the direction whence they had come.

"How many?" demanded Elk's Foot.

The runner held up one hand, with all the digits extended, then held them both up.

"So, there's fifteen," Ralph thought, "more than a match for the three and twenty savages in a fair fight."

True he did once think of joining with his captors, and making a strong resistance, but he relinquished the idea; not even to save his life would he join with the enemies of his people.

"What are you going to do?" he demanded of Elk's Foot, seeing that the individual in question seemed quite complacent over the news.

"What warriors do but fight?" was the sententious rejoinder, in the calmest of tones.

The march was again taken up, in single file, and continued until the natives reached a swampy creek, which was bordered by a dense willow-copse. A narrow passage-way extended several yards across a marshy plat, lined all the way by impenetrable masses of willows. Through this they passed, and kept on for some distance, then turned upon their course, and entered the thickest of the willows, where in a short time every one was effectually screened from sight.

Only Ralph and a single attendant were directed to pursue the route toward the Indian country with all possible despatch. The young man was glad of this for more than one reason. It would spare him the necessity of witnessing the conflict, and if the Indians should by any chance be defeated, he would not fall into the power of his fellow-settlers. So far as being overtaken was concerned, he had no fears, feeling satisfied that he could distance any number of pursuers, when the stake was so important as life or death.

For a short distance Ralph endeavoured to draw his swarthy companion into conversation, but that personage was remarkably reserved. He realized very well that he had been intrusted with an important mission, and he would not allow his charge to escape him by any stratagem. The prisoner understood the motives and feelings of his conductor, and he resolved to play upon them, in case any sounds of conflict were heard behind them.

They had not passed more than half a mile in this manner, when a yell and a volley burst upon their ears. Both paused, as if by mutual consent. But though they listened intently, neither of them was able to decide how the battle was going. A confused firing and shouting reached their ears, but nothing beyond that. Whether the cries came from whites or Indians was a mystery.

Presently a single savage appeared, dashing wildly through the forest. The first glimpse of him convinced Ralph that the settlers had been victorious, and that the Indians were fleeing for life. To his surprise, the guard who had charge of him stood quiet, awaiting the coming of the fleeing brave, though the latter made desperate signals for them to push on.

"Why don't you run!" demanded Ralph. "Your people are defeated. I am going," he added, seeing the fellow did not stir.

"Me shoot!" exclaimed the savage.

"Shoot me! You daren't do it. You'd better lose your head!" returned Ralph, confidently.

C

The savage looked surprised, then turned reluctantly from the spot, and started into a careless run. A race began which it was no easy matter to stop, since he had no authority to shoot the hunter, and to put hand upon him was utterly out of the question. The Indian was hugely perplexed. He made every demonstration which he felt could influence the white to stop, all of which delayed his own progress, and produced no effect upon the runner.

Having led the Indians a race of two or three miles, and demonstrated his ability to distance them upon equal ground, Ralph finally slackened his pace, and allowed them to gain his side. He reasoned that if the Indians were defeated, of which there was no doubt, the settlers would give over the pursuit, upon finding that he was not with them. But if the pursuit should be continued, the vantage-ground he had already gained would be sufficient —he could easily evade them.

Selecting a spot which commanded a tolerably wide view through the forest, the Indians paused, and awaited the re-assembling of their forces. One after another, five or six came in—among them Elk's Foot, the chief of the party. Then came one or two more, bleeding from wounds received in the conflict. And that was all. Eight of twenty-three only remained to tell the sorrowful tale to their people !

With saddened faces their march was resumed, and continued rapidly till the sun was sinking low. The wounded savages, being weakened by loss of blood, were compelled to fall behind, and were soon lost sight of altogether.

Ralph endeavoured to draw from Elk's Foot some of the particulars in regard to the fight, and although that personage was somewhat reserved, he finally succeeded in gaining the details.

It seemed that the whites had sent a single man forward to spy the land in advance of them, and hunt for the Indian trail wherever it might seem doubtful. The scout had noticed the willows, and at once suspected an ambuscade. Making a circuit to the rear of the position, he saw the scalp-lock of a brave waving above the bushes. To send a bullet through the betrayed head was his first act, and one which gave the signal for a general fight. The Indians poured in a fire upon such of their foes as were within sight, but without much effect. They rose up as it was given, and received a withering volley from the whites. As the latter took to trees or threw themselves upon the ground, they presented no certain aim for the Indians, whose willow thicket was little protection against the powerful rifles of their foes. In a very few minutes the savages were so decimated that they simultaneously abandoned the conflict, and fled for dear life. The little band which was now pushing through the wilderness showed how fatal the battle had been.

Near sunset the party halted, built a fire, ate such food as they had with them, set a watch, and threw themselves upon the ground to sleep.

It seemed to Ralph that he had but just begun to doze when he was awakened by a rough hand upon his shoulder, and the voice of Elk's Foot said :—

" Come, pale-face. We go on now."

Rousing himself, he saw that the party was already prepared for a start. The wounded Indians had come up, and were replenishing the fire, as they intended to stay there during the night. The light of day had gone, and only the pale, watching stars remained to guide the savages upon their course. These, however, were quite sufficient, since they were well acquainted with the country through which their route lay, and a very little practice enables the forester, as well as the warrior, to steer his course perfectly by the lesser lights of night.

Hour after hour they travelled, through the long night, till morning began to flush the east. Though they had not hastened, the progress of the party had been steady and uninterrupted. Consequently they must have put many miles between them and Forest Valley during the twenty-four hours of almost constant travel. Ralph did not think the total could be much less than fifty miles, probably not much more than that.

With the first dawning of light the party threw themselves upon the ground, and were soon sleeping soundly; for, though hungry as well as tired, they had no food, and appetite could be best subdued by sleep. Ralph did not immediately submit to the drowsy god, for his brain was whirling with excitement. Hopes and fears alternated. Hopes that he should yet stand forth to the gaze of his fellow-men vindicated and honoured—fears that the terrible crime was too deeply fastened upon him, or that his life might be sacrificed before the consummation of his hopes. His mind was not a little exercised in regard to the experience which awaited him with the Indians. That he was not thus strangely treated without some good reason, was evident. But reflect as he would, no key to the mystery came to his mind. He imagined many possible causes, but none of them seemed probable. However, he could only wait and wonder, and while thus engaged he fell asleep.

He was awakened by some uncomfortable dream, and upon looking up he saw that the hot sun was shining full

in his face. He would have sought a more comfortable
position and resumed his slumbers, of which he felt the
need sorely, but saw that the Indians were already astir,
and making preparations to resume their journey.

Feeling thirsty, Ralph proceeded toward the spring,
near which the Indians had bivouacked. It was surrounded by a dense bushy covert, which it was necessary
to penetrate in order to reach the water.

The hunter was pushing them aside, when he heard
that deadly note of warning—a sharp rattle accompanied
by a hiss! Knowing that he had disturbed the repose of
a deadly serpent, Ralph sought to retreat, but only made
matters worse. His foot came in contact with the loath-
some creature, and the next moment he felt the sharp
fangs buried in his leg!

With a horrified cry he sprung back; the savages who
were nearest him giving vent to louder and more distress-
ing yells. The rattlesnake still clung to the wound,
whipping the earth with his tail, and continuing the
frightful rattles.

The savages seemed petrified with fear, all save Elk's
Foot, who quickly sprung to the rescue of his charge.
With a single blow of his knife he severed the serpent's
head, and both portions of the creature fell to the ground.
He then uttered quick directions to one or two of his
braves, who darted away into the forest, running keen
glances along the ground as they went.

Elk's Foot then set himself at work upon the punctures.
His promptness, coolness, and skill certainly saved the
young man's life. Placing Ralph upon his back the
Indian stripped all clothing from over the wound, which
presented only the most simple appearance. With his
keen knife he proceeded to make incisions quite to the

bone where the serpent's fangs had entered. The blood scarcely flowed at all, but the Indian applied his lips, and sucked away vigorously for several minutes.

"That good," he muttered, between breaths. "Me git him all right perty soon. Bite no bad if Injun know how to fix him. Elk's Foot great medicine—keep his brother pale-face from hurt."

There was something really tender in the redskin's manner, but all was so wrapped up in guile and artifice that Ralph knew not what to make of it. Of one thing he was very certain—the savage was not thus careful of him without some special object in view.

Presently the Indian ceased his operations, and regarded the trickling blood in silence for a moment. Then with a satisfied exclamation he stanched the flow, and bathed the wound in water which some of his attendants brought from the spring.

By the time this was done, those who had been despatched into the forest returned with a handful of green leaves. These Elk's Foot seized eagerly, and having chewed them to a poultice, applied them to the wound. An extemporized bandage was then wound about the injured member, and Ralph placed upon his feet.

Although somewhat lamed by the bite and its summary treatment, the young man found that he still could walk quite comfortably, nor did he feel any effects of the poison in his system. Although he had frequently heard that the Indians cured rattlesnake bites, he had never seen such evidence of their skill before. To say that he was gratified at the result, would not express his feelings properly. He was overjoyed—and the dusky savage rose several degrees in his estimation.

A journey of two hours more brought them to a considerable elevation of ground, and from the top of this the Indian settlement was discovered through the trees. It was situated upon the banks of a small stream, in a healthful and pleasant position. There was an air of neatness and refinement about the place which Ralph had not looked for, and which was certainly unusual in an Indian settlement.

The first impression was not dispelled upon their approach, and although the good taste of the hunter would have suggested many improvements, he was too tired to heed any such trifles now. Squaws and pappooses flocked forth to meet the returning warriors, but the first ardent joy they experienced was checked by the tidings which reached their ears. Of those who had so lately gone forth only the little handful before them had returned! Ralph fancied that many a vengeful glance was cast toward him as the women retreated, tearing their hair and wailing loudly.

The party halted in the midst of the village; food was brought out, and readily disposed of. When Ralph had eaten his fill, Elk's Foot conducted him to a small cabin, built with something of elegance, and opening the door signified that the white was to enter.

The latter could not choose but obey, and when he had crossed the threshold the door was closed and fastened behind him. Truly, he was a prisoner!

Discovering a couch of skins in one corner of the apartment, the desire for rest overcame all other feelings, and he was soon sleeping soundly.

CHAPTER V.

A PRINCESS' WOOING.

RALPH slept several hours, the sun being low in the west when he awoke. For a moment he felt really alarmed. His mouth was dry and parched, a dull pain had settled in his head, and the wounded limb felt sore and stiff. He raised himself to a sitting posture, then stepped upon the floor and moved to a narrow opening which served something of the purpose of a window. These movements convinced him he was not seriously ill. Probably the faint working of the poison had passingly deranged his system, but after the time which had already passed there was no danger of serious results.

Moving back to the couch he sat down, and gave himself up to reflection. All was silent within the cabin, around and without. Still no solution to the mystery of his present position. Several times he rose, walked back and forth a few times, and then sat down again. The idea of passing another night in suspense was far from agreeable.

Just as he was getting nervous over the loneliness of his situation he heard some one unfastening the door, and Elk's Foot stood in his presence. He bore a wooden slab, tolerably well laden with edibles, which he deposited upon a block of wood in the cabin.

"Elk's Foot, I want to know why I'm here?" Ralph demanded, without any ceremony.

The Indian pointed to the food he had brought, and indicated with a grunt that that was to be considered first.

"I am not hungry," Ralph said. "I can't eat anything till I know what the meaning of all this is!"

"Try um," returned Elk's Foot. "Hungry brave eat

—do him good. Make him talk wise words in council when him stomach feel good."

Ralph was vexed at this, but he knew the Indian nature too well to entertain any hopes of dissuading the other. Besides there was something of a promise implied to talk in council when the food should have been disposed of. Comforting himself with this idea, the young man rapidly devoured the edibles, which were well prepared and sauced by hunger. This done, he turned anxiously to the young Indian. The latter had remained watching him intently.

"Now me talk," he said, seating himself upon the ground.

The Indian gazed earnestly upon the white man for some moments. Then he commenced, and in his peculiar manner unfolded the designs which had so puzzled the listener.

Divesting the narrative of that clipped and sententious style peculiar to the North American Indian, and the oft-repeated boasts which graced it, the narrative was as follows :—

His tribe was powerful. Its warriors were counted by hundreds, and its towns were numerous. His father, who was old and near the grave, ruled this great tribe, which upon his death would be equally divided between the two children, Elk's Foot and Sleeping Fawn. The latter was a maiden of great beauty, highly cultivated, and versed in all the agreeable Indian arts. To see her was to love her. From far and near distinguished lovers crowded to seek her smiles and love, but she had none to give them. She had seen a noble white hunter, and her heart had gone forth to him. For many moons she had striven to conquer that love which burned within her, but all in vain. She mourned daily, growing thinner and more like the evening shadows, until her brother had been induced to question her in regard to her secret.

At first she had refused to divulge the cause of her sorrow, but after Elk's Foot had sworn that any wish she might express should be granted, Sleeping Fawn had confessed her love for the fair young hunter of the pale-faces. Since nothing could dissuade her, and the brother's word had been pledged, he took a handful of warriors, and set off to seek the young man. His arrival had been most opportune. He had saved the life of the very man his sister loved, and brought him to her unharmed.

For some moments after this recital was ended Ralph sat like one in a vision. The very idea of an Indian princess falling in love with and causing him to be kidnapped was almost incredible. But he did not doubt the story at all. Everything which he had witnessed thus far confirmed the strange story his captor had related.

" But, how does this Sleeping Fawn know that I shall consent to all this?" demanded Ralph, when his surprise had been in a measure overcome. " It seems to me that she and yourself have taken great liberties in the matter. I am not used to being courted in any such way as that."

" Elk's Foot do what he say," was the earnest rejoinder. " Him bring pale hunter—save him life one—two times. That be not enough? He cannot save him a third time."

" I know you saved my life," returned Ralph, who felt embarrassed by the position in which he was thus involuntarily placed. " I feel thankful to you for it, and will always be your friend. But, really, I'm afraid that I shall have to disappoint your sister. I—"

He would have said that his heart was irrevocably given away, but at that moment the uncertain fate of

Nancy Andrews recurred to his memory, and he checked the utterance.

"White man must be careful," said Elk's Foot, with native dignity. "Me have saved him one—two times, but me can't do it any more. Elk's Foot does not rule the tribe."

It did not require any comment to satisfy Ralph as to what was meant by the words he had just heard. If he chose to marry the Indian princess, and become her slave and the servant of her people, he would no doubt be allowed to do so. But if he chose to dissent, and refuse all idea of such a union, the stern old chief Wolf-Slayer would not allow his daughter's feelings to be outraged with impunity.

Neither feature of the case presented seemed satisfactory to the young hunter. He had no intention of wedding an Indian maiden, nor had he any desire to be hurried out of the world while a crime dishonoured his name among his fellow-settlers. To be certain that there was no mistake, he put the question direct to Elk's Foot:

"You mean that if I don't marry your sister, I shall be killed by your people?"

"Sleeping Fawn must say," was the undecided reply. "She have pale-face now—me done all I say."

"You mean that I am her prisoner, and not yours?"

"Ugh."

"And do you think she would kill me if I refused to wed with her?"

"Better not try um. Sleeping Fawn is proud—she could not live in scorn. Pale-face marry her, and be chief of the great people."

There was silence for some moments, when Elk's Foot rose to his foot

" Now me go," he said. " You sleep good to-night, and in the morning me see you ag'in. Sleeping Fawn see you, too."

" Perhaps she will, and perhaps not," mused Ralph, as the door closed upon him. " I may conclude not to put up at this place much longer."

For the moment he really entertained an idea of trying to escape during the night, but upon second thoughts he abandoned it. His limbs were stiff and swollen, he had no food, or the means of procuring it; and even if he should succeed in leaving the place, it would be next to impossible for him to make any progress in his crippled state. If overhauled and brought back, it might fare worse with him than if he remained. Besides, where would he go ? A return to Forest Valley would insure his death, in all probability. To attempt any longer journey would be simple madness.

After reflecting upon the matter fully, he resolved to await the events of the morrow. Possibly there might be something of hope for him, after all.

Darkness had settled over the face of earth some time previously, and after peering out into the gloom for awhile, Ralph threw himself upon the really comfortable couch, and mused upon his strange situation till sleep visited his eyelids.

During the night he waked frequently, but his exhausted frame required more rest, and he as often relapsed into slumber again. Finally, morning light began to throw the walls of his apartment into relief, and then he rose from the couch.

He was pleased to find that much of the lameness and pain of the evening previous had been allayed by the sound sleep which he had experienced, and after pacing up and down the apartment for some minutes he began to feel a longing for freedom. He even felt that he could distance any of his pursuers in a dead race through the forest.

But it would be more than difficult for him to get outside the hut which contained him, since it could hardly have been stronger if built for a prison. The only outlet through which a man could pass was the door, and that was effectually fastened upon the outside.

While he was engaged in pacing back and forth, reflecting, or endeavouring to reflect, upon the strange situation in which he was placed, the fastenings of the door were removed, and Elk's Foot stepped into the room, bearing a quantity of food.

Ralph's first impression was to throw himself upon the Indian as he opened the door, and burst forth; but the very thought of it was so unreasonable that he refrained, and welcomed the savage heir to a half tribe with something like a smile. The Indian noticed this, and a glow of unmistakable pleasure mantled his features. Placing the food upon the block, as he had done previously, the savage pointed toward it, saying :—

" Eat. Me come back pretty soon with Sleeping Fawn."

As he thus spoke the uncivilized match-maker retreated, and the sounds of his footsteps soon died away along the street.

The fact that he was to be visited by the damsel whose affections he had so unwittingly captivated, did not tend to restore Ralph's equanimity. But, as there was no assistance, he concluded to act the wiser part, and attacked the viands with commendable zeal.

His appetite was satisfied, and nearly an hour had

passed without bringing the expected visitors. How to meet them was a question which he could not contemplate with satisfaction. Of one thing he felt sure. Time must be gained, if possible.

At length footsteps sounded without, and neared the door. His heart beat somewhat irregularly at the thought of the trial at hand. But, nerving himself with an effort, he awaited their coming.

Elk's Foot entered first, and when he was within the apartment a female figure glided in. For some moments the parties stood regarding each other in silence. Then Sleeping Fawn whispered to her brother in the language of the tribe, which was entirely strange to Ralph.

Had the young man never met with Nancy Andrews, or even had he been less firm in his moral convictions, it is quite possible that the Indian maiden's enterprise might not have been in vain. Candidly, it appeared to him that he never had seen a form more lovely than the one which now stood before him. Her features were regular and faultlessly beautiful, while the sparkle of intelligence and love gleamed in her deep hazel eyes.

To be the object of such passionate affection from such a source might well have turned the brain of a man whose years had been spent in the wild freedom of the forest; more especially when it was considered that she was a princess in her own right. But Ralph had taken his stand, and his studied reserve must have been plainly apparent to the lovely Sleeping Fawn. She gazed fixedly at him for a moment, then her eyes drooped with an expression of sadness quite touching.

"Sleeping Fawn would wed the pale-face," said her brother, briefly. "She has come for his answer."

This was certainly putting the question bluntly—a

trifle more so than Ralph had expected. For a moment he hesitated how to reply.

" What if I will, and what if I don't choose to ?" he finally asked, hoping to learn more positively of their intentions.

" If he will, me love him, and pale-face rule over my people," said Sleeping Fawn, who spoke English with a purer intonation than her brother. " He shall be great man in the councils of the Indians. Everybody love him, and braves delight to go on war-path with him."

" That is if I will," said Ralph. " Now what if I do not wish to ?"

The maiden gazed a moment. Her reason told her very plainly that he did not wish anything of the kind, but love was still strong in her bosom.

" If he will not," she said, finally, " me hate !"

The tone in which she spoke left no room for doubt. She had loved violently, and no pains had been spared to gain possession of her love's object. If that love was scorned, it would be but natural that she should hate as intently, and in that case the young man realised how precarious his position must be.

" You will give me time—till to-night, at least, to think of this ?" he said.

Not that he would be any better adapted to meet the result twelve hours hence than at the present time. But his main idea was to gain time, and if that could be accomplished, other events might work with advantage to him.

" You had time to think," said Elk's Foot.

" But I am not decided," was the reply. " I must have more time—must see your place and people."

" Pale-face can think very well here !" was the decided

answer, and almost contrary to his expectations the
brother and sister retired, leaving him alone to ponder
over the unenviable situation.

CHAPTER VI

LOVE AND HATE.

For some time Ralph Rilley sat upon the couch of
skins and pondered. Perhaps he had only made matters
worse by his delay. Why did he not ask for longer
grace, to consider the matter and plan for escape?
Possibly he might, even now, gain time till the following
morning, and during the night some possibility might
present for getting free. He had hoped that more
freedom would be granted him during the day, but the
parting words of Elk's Foot had satisfied him that such
would not be the case.

It was near noon, perhaps a little past, when that re-
doubtable warrior reappeared, bearing more food, and
disposed for further "talk" with Ralph. Hoping to
learn more of the savage's intentions toward him, the
young man readily seated himself, and a parley of considerable length ensued. Its results were far from
satisfactory

The Indian could harp upon but one theme—gratitude
for the favour he had rendered the white man. Surely
this should be sufficient reason for the latter marrying
his sister. In vain Ralph urged that he had not been
granted time to study the character and disposition of
the lady he was expected to wed. All his arguments
were turned aside by the shrewd Indian, however often
repeated.

The conference broke up at length, and Elk's Foot took

his departure, neither feeling more satisfied for the talk. Ralph began really to feel alarmed. Not even when in the hands of the mob had he felt himself in that danger which was about him now. It was sufficient that he was in the hands of the untutored, capricious savages, and that the choice had been presented him between living or a speedy death. It was hard for him to die, thus, in his early manhood—especially hard to leave behind a name to which the foulest of human crimes clung! But it seemed preferable to dishonour. Nay, he reflected until it really seemed that 'twere easy to die with a pure conscience.

Through the long afternoon such thoughts as these filled his mind, and when the lengthened shades of evening came they found him firm. If he could not obtain further time, he would boldly declare against the desired marriage, and brave the issues!

Even sooner than he expected, the party came. Elk's Foot led the way, as before, followed by Sleeping Fawn. The rear was brought up by a tall savage, of dignified mien, though far advanced in life, wrinkled and scarred. This Ralph at once concluded to be Wolf-Slayer, the mighty chief of the powerful tribe. The trio advanced to the midst of the cabin, Elk's Foot closing and fastening the door behind them.

"The pale-face is a great warrior, and is wise!" began Sleeping Fawn. "His heart has learned wisdom. He will rule over the half of the great tribe of which the Wolf-Slayer is king!"

She indicated the tall savage beside her, who grunted as his name was mentioned.

"The Sleeping Fawn has said well," the old chief responded. "But she is weak. She does not love her own people, but begs a pale-face to rule her tribe. It is well. The pale-face cannot refuse, for her heart is set upon him."

There was a grunt from each of the three, and from their manner Ralph inferred that they awaited his reply. He still had some hopes of gaining time, and it was with this purpose he commenced :—

"I have not seen the people belonging to the Wolf-Slayer's tribe. I do not know much of the Sleeping Fawn. I have not learned to love her. It requires time for a white man to learn such things, and he must see the maiden of his choice often, and in her daily works."

The savages listened patiently, for they would not interrupt him, but when he had ceased speaking the chief replied :—

"Who loves the Wolf-Slayer's daughter? Is it not enough that she loves the pale-face and has saved his life? Let him marry her soon, and learn love in the long summer moons !"

"But, that is not the custom of my people," returned Ralph ; "I could not do so. I must learn to love first—then I may marry."

"The pale-face is to be pale-face no more," retorted the head chief, speaking almost perfect English, and using very decided movements. "He must be Injun—or nothing."

"But I cannot change in a moment," persisted Ralph. "I must have time. You cannot deny me that, surely?"

The chief uttered a grunt of impatience.

"The pale-face talk well," he said—"make great man among the Injuns. Wolf-Slayer want him for son. Can have him? Sleeping Fawn is impatient—she would know."

" When will the marriage take place ?"

" Now. Another sun must see him the husband of Sleeping Fawn !"

" No, not so soon as that," said Ralph, decidedly.

" Must be."

" It shall not be—I will not be married thus hastily !" the fearless hunter declared.

" To-night or never the pale-face must wed Sleeping Fawn !" declared the chief.

" Then it shall be never !" was the unequivocal answer.

The trio of savages seemed somewhat startled at this bold declaration, and the disappointed maiden uttered a low cry, as of despair. Rage and mortification appeared to blend in the visages of the men. For some moments not a person in the cabin moved—the three Indians gazing upon the daring white who had scorned their greatest boon, and he as steadily returning their gaze.

Suddenly the Indian maiden drew a sharp knife from its place of concealment, and with a cry of rage threw herself upon Ralph, endeavouring to plunge the weapon into his body.

Although the act was unlooked for, the young man was not taken entirely at a disadvantage. He had more than half expected such an onset from the father or brother, and was only surprised that the daughter should seek her own revenge.

Grasping the hand which held the weapon, he gave way as she came on, and very soon had the knife in his own hand. The maiden turned away with a sob, realising that she was in no danger from the man whose life she had sought.

For a moment it seemed that the control of the place was to change hands. Ralph had the knife, and with it in hand he rushed towards the door. But Elk's Foot uttered a loud cry, and remained stationary, as did his father and sister.

Ralph succeeded in opening the door, but here he was confronted by a couple of Indians, armed with guns. They quickly covered his person with their pieces, and ordinary prudence induced him to retreat. Seeing that any offensive act must certainly cost his life, he hurled the knife through one of the openings, and with folded arms awaited the action of his savage guards. That they were his foes now could not be doubted. But it was possible that they might temporise for a while, and there his only hope rested.

Elk's Foot stepped to the door, and called one of the Indians inside, giving him orders to watch Ralph closely, and shoot him at the first movement. Hearing the substance of this charge, the young man seated himself upon the couch of skins, while the sentinel cocked and pointed his gun, in readiness to obey the order most literally.

The three great powers of the tribe then gathered in one corner, and discussed the matter, apparently at great length. The result of their deliberations was not known, but they soon prepared to leave the place, the son repeating certain instructions to the savage guard, which caused his evil eyes to dance with lively anticipation. He relaxed a trifle in fierceness, however, and when the door was shut and fastened upon the outside, seemed to fancy that the prisoner was secure, without any especial watchfulness upon his part.

Sunset came, faded away into twilight, and that in turn into darkness. Still they remained undisturbed in the cabin. No supper had been brought to Ralph, but he was not especially in need of it, and finally settled back upon the couch, not to sleep, but to think and plot.

He was far from relishing the idea of a night passed in this place, since there could hardly remain the shadow of a hope for him, should daylight come and find him within those walls. But how to leave? No doubt, that could be managed if he were freed from the presence of any looker-on; but there was the guard, a bloodthirsty Indian, who had been designated expressly to watch him, and foil any attempt to escape. Beyond this, the door was fastened upon the outside, and very likely the place might be guarded without, in addition to the sentinel within.

Surely the prospect was dark enough, and any man less determined than Ralph Rilley would have succumbed to the force of circumstances brought against him. He, however, felt that life was worth a desperate effort, and while the Indian supposed him to be asleep or thinking over his fate of the morrow, he was really meditating in what manner he should break the chain of influences binding him beneath that fatal roof.

Silently the hours passed, and midnight was near at hand. The sentry had drawn the block of wood beside the couch whereon his charge slept, as he supposed, and sat upon it, half dozing. The prisoner was fully aware of this, for although the darkness was nearly impenetrable, he exerted every sense to the utmost. Gradually, inch by inch, fraction by fraction, the reclining form was drawing nearer, noting every movement of the sentinel, and waiting for an opportunity to spring upon him for a death-struggle. If the young man's life was to end soon, it might as well be in a struggle with the Indian before him as in any more hideous manner.

One of the most difficult tricks imaginable is that of

maintaining strict watch through the long hours of night, with nothing, not even the power of movement, to keep the senses active. To sit and watch a motionless figure, hour in and hour out, with no motion or sound to stir the mind of the watcher, is one of the severest forms of this severe task. Thus it was that, though the Indian struggled strongly with the drowsiness which visited his lids, they would close, almost in spite of him. Momentarily the feeling gained ground, and just at the time when Ralph ceased his motions, and began to watch for indications of temporary forgetfulness upon the part of his guard, the latter's grasp upon his gun relaxed, and the barrel slipped from his fingers. Quickly he grasped for it, but another hand had been quicker, and already the weapon was in the possession of Ralph.

As one sprung to his feet, the other did the same. Ralph swung the gun through the air and endeavoured to strike the Indian, but the latter rushed forward and grappled the white around the body, feeling confusedly for his knife. The musket fell upon the floor, the stock being broken from the barrel by the concussion. Then commenced a desperate struggle for the savage's knife, the only weapon in the cabin.

Their struggle was necessarily confined to narrow limits. Directly behind Ralph was the couch, behind the Indian the block upon which he had been sitting. The question seemed to be which could push the other backward, and thus gain the fall. Brace and push was at once the order of the struggle, and in the tussle which followed, neither had a hand to lend for the knife.

In such a conflict few men could stand against Ralph Rilley, and, though fighting for life, the Indian was not one of those few. Gradually his bracing position was lost, his limbs touched the block, and the struggle was ended. He had not even time to utter the cry which trembled upon his lips ere Ralph had caught him by the throat, and both came to the ground, the white uppermost.

That iron grip was not relaxed till all struggles and tremors on the Indian's part ceased, and then but slowly, as Ralph feared deception. He need have entertained no doubts. No human being could have lived without breathing for that length of time. Satisfied that all was over, the victor unbuckled his adversary's belt, and strapped it about himself, retaining his knife. Then he felt for the musket, but it was broken beyond all repair. What should he do next?

This was a serious question. He already had taken human life as an incipient step, and having gone thus far it was impossible to recede. He knew the door to be fastened, consequently he must seek other means of escape. But one plan seemed to give any promise—that was, to dig out, beneath the foundations of the cabin. The structure had no floor but the smoothly-trodden ground, and rested upon four beams of timber placed prone upon the earth.

Though the operation of tunneling out would require some time, it seemed the only mode practicable, and Ralph set about it without any unnecessary delay. By dint of continued exertion, he soon created an opening sufficiently large to admit of his passage to the outer world; though in so doing he completely ruined the knife, the only weapon, as well as the only tool, he could procure.

This done, he satisfied himself that the way was clear without, before venturing from the cabin. No one seemed stirring—a universal quiet reigned over the village. A light, drizzling rain was setting in, which was certainly in his favour, as he had no firearms to suffer from the dampness, and even Indians would be less likely to prowl about upon such a night. There was the disadvantage, however, that he had not even the pale stars as guides, and was liable to wander from a direct course, or even to lose the proper direction altogether.

Yet his heart was by no means faint, and after passing through a portion of the village, he struck off into the trackless forest. Morning could not be far distant, and until that time he would trust to chance and his natural skill as a hunter. Filled with hope, and buoyed up by the natural vigour of his spirits, Ralph pushed on, regardless of the many obstacles in his way.

CHAPTER VII.

A MAN HUNT.

THE terrible excitement in Forest Valley had given place to mourning. Nearly one-fourth of the able-bodied men had passed from earth during that night of terror. In the years that had transpired since the founding of the settlement only one death, that of a child, had taken place. It will be easy to imagine the dismay caused by such a wholesale filling up of the little graveyard.

The fallen ones had been consigned to their last rest, and the mourners had returned to their homes. A terrible pall brooded over the pleasant village. Young and old moved about with subdued tread, and only spoke in the saddest of voices concerning the great tragedy which had been enacted in their midst. The prosperous life of Forest Valley had been suddenly changed in its tone, and even some of the more timid began to think

seriously of abandoning the work of years, and returning
again to the more populous regions.

It was night—a week later than that fearful night on
which they had awakened to such a multiplicity of
horrors. The family of Stephen Rilley—Ralph's brother,
with whom he had resided—was sleeping soundly.

Suddenly, in the dead of night, Rilley and his wife
heard a gentle rapping upon the window of their apartment.

" Who's there ? " was the abrupt demand.

" Ask no questions, but let me in," said a voice which
they at once recognized.

" Ralph has come—he is alive ! " said both, in glad
tones.

Stephen sprung to the door, and opened without any
ceremony. Ralph entered, and barely grasped the hand
extended to him before sinking into a chair.

" I am very tired, Stephen," he said. "I have scarcely
eaten anything for three days. Cannot you give me a
cold bite ?—anything to stay the pangs of hunger for a
time ? "

" Certainly, my brother," returned Stephen, warmly.
' Even if I believed you guilty of the crime which stands
charged to you, I should not refuse to give you food and
shelter."

" As God is my witness, I am not guilty ! " said Ralph.

" I know it—I believe it," was the earnest response.
' Come this way, and we will soon provide for your needs."

He led the way into an adjoining room, which was
used as a kitchen, and placed before the needy one an
abundance of food. The latter addressed himself to the
viands for some time, to the exclusion of all conversation,
but finally he gazed up at his brother, and asked :—

" Has anything been learned yet regarding the murder, or the whereabouts of Nancy Andrews ? "

Stephen shook his head.

" Nothing has transpired to throw the least light upon the affair. Of course, the coming of the Indians was all attributed to you, and many impossible stories have been told and gained ground, till most of the people really believe anything, no matter how absurd."

" And they all think me guilty ? "

" Very nearly. Those who were opposed to your being hung at once only wished to wait for daylight and additional proofs—scarcely a man beyond this house but believes you murdered Jehonikam Andrews. Some of the women profess to think you innocent, or rather that you only did it in self-defence, but they do not speak of it very freely. You always were a favourite among the ladies, Ralph ! "

" But what connexion do they suppose I could have had with the savages ? "

" The story most generally believed, with many modifications and variations, is that you induced Nancy away from her house, or forcibly abducted her, and placed her in charge of the Indians, who were to take care of her, and to rescue you if there was any danger. They professed to think that you had gone to the Indian country with your bride, whether married or not, and that we never should see you again."

" Not so far from right as might have been ! " laughed the outcast.

" May I ask where you have been ? " said Stephen, who was somewhat perplexed by his brother's manner. " I trust you are not afraid to confide in me."

Just then Stephen's wife, who had risen and dressed

hastily, entered the apartment. She advanced to Ralph and greeted him warmly, showing beyond any doubt that she did not think him guilty, whatever others might do.

"Where have you been, Ralph, during all this dreadful week which has passed?" she asked.

"Just what he was about to tell," returned her husband. "Sit down, Kate, and we will listen, for I know my brother too well to think for a moment that he would tell anything but the truth."

"Thank you for the good opinion," remarked Ralph. "I have no reason to tell you anything else. I am innocent of any crime."

He then gave them a concise but clear account of all that had happened, from the time he had lost or rather regained consciousness after the attempt at hanging, till he regained his freedom, and started upon the return toward home.

"I knew no other course to take," he said, in conclusion. "I felt that possibly Nancy had been discovered, dead or alive. In any case it seemed to me that some revelations must have taken place during the time I had been absent. But if I found that the crime still attached to me, I could get my rifle and pistols, and then take to the woods again. I could lie in wait there till something should happen to prove my innocence—for it will be proved, sooner or later, though I may not live to see the day.

"When morning came I found that I had wandered to some place unknown to me. In which direction I had been travelling was a mystery. I neither knew which way the Indian village lay, nor how far I might be from it. Still I could shape my course by the sun, and the idea of freedom gave me strength to travel with my usual speed. I walked till exhausted, and sat down to rest—I was hungry, but could find no food, nor had I any means of killing the wild game which I saw occasionally. But 1 did not mind this. My good luck would scarcely let me starve to death, and the pangs of hunger were much more tolerable than roasting at an Indian fire.

"Presently I began to fear pursuit. Why, I scarcely knew. There was a tolerable eminence before me, and gaining the top of it, I found that I had command of the country as far as the eye could reach through the forest. I had not lain in this position more than five minutes, when I saw the form of an Indian through the woods. Others appeared behind him, and I knew they were in pursuit of me.

"As I had no means of fighting them, my only safety lay in flight. I calculated that they were eighty rods distant, and this distance gave me a tolerable start. In ordinary times I would not have asked for this advantage, but I had found that my bitten leg was not entirely sound, and I knew not how seriously it might trouble me in a long race.

"For two miles I ran vigorously, and up to this time the Indians had not caught sight of me, though they had my fresh tracks to guide them. At this time I came to a long, level stretch of land, upon which the trees, though of great size, grew very sparsely. I did not notice this fact till I had entered upon it, perhaps could not have avoided it if seen.

" I had almost gained a roll of ground at the opposite side, and was straining every nerve to compass that object, when the Indians caught a glimpse of me. With fierce shouts and yells they came on, and although I had gained somewhat upon them thus far, I saw that they must eventually run me down. Unless I could hit upon some method for throwing them off the track, I felt that all was up with me.

"I did not abate my speed, as that would have been certainly fatal. My good luck was uppermost. At the distance of eighty or a hundred rods I saw a water-course. If I could reach that, I felt there was hope for me. Possibly I could enter the water, and thus divert them from my track.

"Exerting every muscle to the utmost, I soon gained the banks of the stream, and plunged in. Looking back I saw that none of the savages were yet in sight. Turning up the brook I walked rapidly, and soon gained a point where the banks were high and overgrown with dense masses of juniper bushes. Under these I found abundant shelter, the banks in many places being hollowed out by the action of the water, to a considerable depth. Gaining one of the water-built caverns, I waited to notice the action of the savages.

"On reaching the water they suspected that I had not crossed in that place. Probably they saw my tracks going down, but none coming up on the other side. There was scarcely a dozen of them, but it was far from a pleasant sensation on my part to see them coming directly up the stream. I had supposed they would go downward, but their noses or some other sense must have directed them toward me. On they came, a portion upon either bank of the stream. I was somewhat relieved at finding that they only looked for my tracks, though I could not suppose they would pass the bushes without giving them a thorough overhauling. But they seemed to have no idea that I had stopped in the vicinity They merely examined the borders of the creek upon a run, glancing all around to see if I was in sight through the trees.

"After going up some distance above my hiding-place they returned, galloping and shouting, and soon disappeared down the creek. It was a question with me whether to remain where I was, or continue my way. I might be discovered in any case, but I felt the safer way was to make the best time I could toward home. I climbed out cautiously, and hearing their shouts a long way off, I bent my course over the hills at a rate which soon removed the extra water from my clothing.

"I gave them the slip, and succeeded in escaping their observation. They followed me during the day, frequently getting ahead of me, but I always managed to elude them. Once, indeed, a single savage espied me, and called to his followers, but I turned sharp upon my course, and left them bewildered and discomfited. There the chase must have ended, for I saw them no more.

"I have been lying about in the woods for several hours, not caring to come in till the inhabitants should all be asleep. I must not stay longer. Let me get my weapons, and then I can live in the forest, harming nobody and afraid of nobody. Sooner or later this mystery will be cleared up, and then I can come back and be your brother again, openly."

"You will at least lay down and sleep a few hours," urged Kate, who felt all a sister's interest in the noble young man. "We will wake you before light, so that there can be no danger."

"No, no, Kate; I must not stay. I can sleep perfectly well in the forest, and when I have means of procuring food and defending myself from Indians, I can live very well till such time as I am proved innocent."

Stephen had passed from the apartment, but soon came back, bringing the rifle and pistols, with a quantity of ammunition.

"Your powder-horn was nearly empty," he said, holding up the one he had brought; "so I took mine, which was almost full. There's near a hundred bullets in your pouch, and when either gets reduced come to me, I shall always have a supply.

Ralph thanked his brother, and took the ammunition, which he quickly disposed of. Then he slipped the pistols into his belt, and slung the rifle over his shoulder.

"Now I feel like a man again!" he exclaimed. "Lend me one of your knives, Stephen, for I have nothing to cut my food with, as I spoiled this thing digging out of the Indian cabin."

He threw down the battered Indian blade as he spoke, and Stephen sprung to bring the required article. In a moment he re-entered the apartment, saying, hurriedly:—

"The house is being surrounded, Ralph; I fear all is discovered! You must hide quickly, or they will find you."

"Never fear for me. Do you be abed and fast asleep. I will take care of myself! Go—you know nothing as to where I am—I have been here, but am gone."

There was something in his manner so impressive to the hearers that they could not refuse compliance, and immediately stole from the room. No sooner were they gone than Ralph slipped into the chimney, and was soon hidden from ordinary observation.

He had scarcely vacated the apartment when a loud knock resounded upon the door. Stephen now gathered more fully his brother's meaning, and in a drowsy tone asked who was there.

" Never mind," was the savage response.   " Open the
door; we want that murderer that's in here !"

" There is no murderer here," said Stephen Rilley.

" Never mind.   Open the door, or down it comes, this
very minit !"

As Stephen was already dressed he fumbled about for
a moment, and then opened the door, looking exceedingly
sleepy.

" I don't see what you mean disturbing a man at this
time o' night," he said, rather petulantly.

But no heed was paid to his words, and the excited
rabble rushed into the rooms, overthrowing chairs and
table, and grasping imaginary foes in every corner.
Lights were soon produced, and then William Rufus,
who had ever been foremost in the endeavours to sacra-
fice Ralph, presented a pistol at Rilley's head.

" We want to know whar' that murderer is !" he said,
in tones intended to be very impressive.

" That is something I cannot tell you," replied the
threatened man.   " I do not know."

" D'ye mean to say that Ralph Rilley hain't been here
to-night !"

" He has been here, but is gone," said Stephen, recollecting the parting charge of his brother.

" When did he go ?—which way ?—and where?"

" I do not know."

" Remember this pistol "—and the muzzle was brought
still closer to his head.

" I see it," returned Stephen, " but I tell you only the
truth.   I do not know where he is.   You are at liberty
to examine the house and look for him where you choose."

" Don't waste time," shouted another.   " He is in this
house, I tell you ; let's find him."

"So we will, boys," said Rufus. "Take one room at a time, and make sure of it."

CHAPTER VIII.

THE SEARCH.

THE plan was quickly carried out. One room after another was closely examined, and every cranny underwent the strictest scrutiny. The cellar, chamber, and chimney were respectively peered into, and no box or barrel left unturned. Yet, when the party reassembled in the room whence the search had started, they were forced to confess that it had been utterly fruitless.

Stephen Rilley had anxiously awaited the result, hoping that his brother might escape. Rufus now approached him, and the pistol was again brought into requisition.

"Where is that fellow?" he demanded, brandishing the weapon. "You know where he is, now, don't deny it; 'tmay be the wuss for ye, in the end."

"I told you he was gone," replied Stephen, calmly. "You found my words true."

"But I tell you we know he hain't left this house. He's here somewhere, and we want him."

"You've my permission to search the house. I know no more than you what has become of him. He has left —that is all I know."

"He hain't gone, I tell you—the house has been watched ever since we found out he was here. Have you looked in the chimney?"

The last remark was addressed to one of his followers, who was especially active in the search. The person questioned ran to the chimney, peered up, and even ascended a few steps.

D

"Confound it all, Bill," he muttered, sliding to the floor, and brushing off the soot, "I can't tell. Seems as if I could see suthin' up thar', but I hain't sure."

A general peering up chimney followed, some going so far as to declare that they could see him plainly, while others seemed far from certain in regard to the matter.

"See here!" exclaimed Rufus, stepping to the bed which had been vacated by Stephen and his wife, "one of you jest throw that straw into the fireplace, while I tell them outside to keep their rifles on top of the chimney; we'll soon bring him down if he is up thar'!"

The men were delighted at the prospect of such rare sport, and filled the ample fireplace with straw, when Rufus stepped to the door, and in loud tones bade those without watch the chimney, and shoot at anyone attempting to leave it. This done, he returned to the room where his followers were assembled, and fire was applied to the combustible mass.

Stephen watched the fierce flames as they shot up with a terrible fear at his heart. He did not think it possible that Ralph could have left the house, and the only place where he could be secreted was there. Every moment he looked to see a smothered form fall to the floor, or to hear the report of rifles without. But the minutes passed, the straw burned out, and all continued silent. The vigilance of the search was all unrewarded, and with a crest-fallen air Rufus turned to his deluded followers.

"He can't be here, we must look som'ers else for him," he said. "But he's som'ers near, and we'll nab him before he can git off."

The searching party bustled out of the house, and were soon scouring about in the vicinity, thinking it possible he might have slipped from the dwelling unobserved.

But they found nothing, and, after venting their disappointment in oaths, proceeded into the forest, rather with a hope than any expectations of finding him.

When they had gained a safe distance from the house, Ralph suddenly emerged in the apartment where Stephen and Kate were standing, wondering what had become of the person in question.

" Where in this world, Ralph, did you hide ?" the brother demanded. " I looked to see you hunted down every moment. Did you go up the chimney ?"

" Yes, there was where I went at first. But before I tell you more, get me the knife we spoke of, so that I can be ready to leave at any time."

Though very anxious to hear how his shrewd and daring brother had escaped, Stephen hastened for the weapon, and soon returned with it in his hand.

" There is a man beneath one of the windows of this room," he said, placing the weapon in Ralph's hand. " I think he is left as a spy. I saw him crawling along and endeavouring to peer in; possibly he heard the sound of your voice."

" That is unlucky," mused Ralph. " If I attempt to leave he will be certain to follow, and bring down the whole crew upon me. I think I can fix him. Let me reflect a moment. I must not hurt him—I have no wish to ; and yet I cannot consent tamely to be hung. I have it, now !"

He went to the cupboard, and taking up a tin box, poured a quantity of its contents into his hand. Then he moved toward another part of the room.

" Come this way," he said, " and I will tell you how I have escaped so far, though I must be in a hurry. When I went up the chimney I stopped on top of the partition,

and concluded I could slip from side to side and dodg
them so. I did that while they were searching the rooms
but when they began to talk of burning me out witl
straw, I concluded that it would not be safe with all mj
powder aboard. I knew by their conversation that all o
them were in this room, and they seemed to have for
gotten that there was any other outlet to the chimney.
So I slid down into the other room, and in the closet
found a secure hiding-place till they had gone. But I
must not stay a moment longer than necessary. Look
out, if you want to see fun !"

" I only wonder what you intend doing with my red
pepper !" said Kate.

" It will be no wonder long," he remarked, descending
the cellar steps.

Having reached the cellar, Ralph proceeded to one of
the windows, which he carefully opened, and gazed forth.
The silent form crouching a few feet distant heard no
sound till the doomed hunter spoke in a changed voice.

" D'ye hear anythin' ?" he almost whispered.

" What d'ye say ?" demanded the watcher.

" D'ye hear anythin' ?"

" Is that you, Jones ?"

" It ain't anybody else."

" No, I don't know's I did," was the hesitating reply,
as the face drew near the cellar window. " I did think I
heern somebody in thar', but a feller can't look in, an' I
guess 'twan't nobody but Steve—"

At that moment his observations came to an end, as
the handful of pepper was dashed into his face, filling his
eyes, nostrils, and mouth with the fine, pungent dust!
The effect was electrical. The unsuspecting victim rolled
upon the ground, coughing, gasping, sneezing, endeavour-

ing to shout, but utterly unable to command the requisite amount of breath.

Ralph merely made sure that his work was effectually done, and then hastened above. He found Stephen and Kate almost convulsed at the ludicrous postures of the suffering spy whom they had watched.

" I haven't hurt him," the young man said, hurriedly. " Now I must say good-bye, for it is uncertain when we may meet again."

A few hasty words of parting were spoken, and then the young man opened the door. Looking carefully forth, to make sure that none of his foes were at hand, he passed into the open air, and soon the darkness hid him from the eyes of his friends.

Not till he reached the darkest shades of the forest did the fugitive pause, and then but for a moment. How to proceed, in what direction to go, and where to pause, were points upon which he could not decide. More fully than ever he realised how utterly outcast he was—how doubly doomed ! The savages sought his life, but sought it no more persistently than did the whites—those with whom he had lived for many years, and during all those years had borne a spotless character. But he reflected that appearances were against him—that it was but natural for his fellows to fix the dreadful crime of murder upon him.

That he could prove his innocence at some time he did not doubt ; yet, meanwhile, he must keep himself concealed, not only from the whites but also from the aborigines. If he was fortunate enough to do this, all would be well.

These thoughts passed through the young man's mind in a moment, and he decided to shape his course to the westward. There he knew game to be plenty, and in those lonely, almost unexplored wilds, he would be comparatively secluded from the world of mankind, red and white.

To think was to act, for he had no time to lose. In what direction his pursuers had gone he hardly knew, but trusted to his good fortune and ready instinct to avoid them, if any chance should throw him in conjunction with them.

Ralph walked very rapidly, for it was verging toward morning, and he wished to put a respectable stretch of wilderness between himself and those who sought his life before light should visit the earth. He knew the region perfectly, and scarcely gave heed to his footsteps, so busy were his thoughts with the strange scenes through which he had passed.

But he was soon brought to consciousness by the appearance of a figure just in advance of him, and the abrupt question :—

" Nothin' of the murderer, I reckin ?"

" No, I don't find anything. Where's the rest of 'em ?"

" Who be you ?" demanded the other, bending forward, and endeavouring to peer into the young man's face. " Well, never mind—the rest are right out this way; come on, I'll take ye to 'em."

" No matter about it," returned Ralph, carelessly. "I'll take a scout off this way, and maybe we'll find something."

" Guess not !" ventured his interloculor, endeavouring to bring his rifle to bear. " You're the very man we want —come along !"

He uttered a loud, quick signal with the same breath, and the fugitive realised that he was getting into a decidedly dangerous position. With the bound of a cat, Ralph sprung upon the other, and bore him to the ground. Then grasping the man's weapon he hurled it away in a direction opposite to the one he intended taking himself.

Meanwhile, the person upon the ground manifested no disposition to remain there. No sooner had Ralph relaxed his hold than he sprung to his feet, only to be knocked down by a powerful blow from the other's fist.

While he was regaining his scattered senses, Ralph was flying rapidly through the woods. He could hear the sounds of gathering forces, and knew that every moment was inestimably precious. There was some confusion when the settlers reached their comrade. All was conjecture as to which way the fugitive had gone.

This matter was decided by that personage himself, who unwittingly plunged into a mass of dry weeds, which cracked and snapped beneath his tread. Before he was really aware of the danger, his own movements had betrayed him. With a shout and a rush the eager man-hunters started in pursuit, some of them stopping to discharge their weapons first. But the balls flew wide, since the darkness gave them no opportunity to aim, and the pursued man sped forward with vigorous bounds.

In a moment the race and pursuit became exciting. The fugitive had no advantage, save that of knowing the forest more thoroughly than any other person in the settlement. But to offset this, the pursuers were fresh and in great numbers ; so that by scattering to the right and left, they prevented Ralph from turning in either direction without great danger of immediate capture.

Occasional shots were fired by those who heard the young man's steps, and fancied that a chance bullet might save them a long run in the dark. But none of them took

effect.   They were fired too hastily, and without any cer-
tainty of aim.

Suddenly the sound of footsteps in advance ceased, and
a glad shout went up from the pursuers.   They had no
doubt but that he had fallen, and with renewed cries they
hastened to the spot, expecting to find his bleeding form
upon the ground.

Very naturally there arose diverse opinions as to the
precise place where the sounds had ceased, more especially
as they found nothing to reward their search in the
vicinity.   From side to side they sped, peering through the
gloom at every object which appeared in dark relief upon
the surface of the earth, and in useless search spent considerable time, disputing and blustering as all bodies of
excited men will do.

Very naturally they came to the conclusion that they
had been deceived throughout, and that the man they
were looking for had employed the time in making good
his escape.   In addition to this gain of time, none knew
the route he had taken, and pursuit under such circumstances would quite as likely be wrong as right.

"Scatter, my boys!" shouted William Rufus, who was
almost frantic at his repeated disappointments.   "Some
of you go in various ways, and the one that finds him fire
his gun as a signal."

The men hastened to obey, and radiated through the
forest in all directions.   As every one was anxious to find
the first traces, knowing it would redound to his con-
sequence and distinction, the efforts of many an earnest
searcher would have been ludicrous in the extreme if
daylight could have rendered them visible.

But, despite all the zeal carried into the search, it proved
fruitless.   Guns were discharged, to be sure, and every

one flocked toward the sound, but it proved a false alarm in every case, and long after daybreak the weary party gave over the blind search, and retired to Forest Valley, weary, hungry, and dissatisfied.

CHAPTER IX.

OLD FRIENDS.

THE race which Ralph led his enemies through the forest, and the manner in which he gave them the slip finally, had all been meditated in the youth's mind from the moment of his setting out. Making all possible noise as he ran, and feeling sure that they were not gaining essentially upon him, he suddenly slackened his speed, and stole away in a different direction. His movements were now as noiseless as they had previously been careless, and it was but natural that the man-hunters should suppose him to have fallen from the effects of a shot. Such was not the result he had anticipated, however, although it answered his purpose admirably. He merely intended to confuse them, and gain a tolerable distance while they were looking for him. This he certainly did, being at least half-a-mile distant before the radiating pursuit was organized. As he did not pause, merely turning his course more to the northward as he progressed, it will be seen how faint the chances for overhauling him were.

At length daylight began to bring out the features of the forest more plainly, and then Ralph changed his course again. He had been obliged to take a direction due northeast at the outset, which had of course taken him almost directly away from the region of his intended sojourn. This course he had gradually changed to one leading north, but this was scarcely better. as. while taking him away from the whites, it was leading toward the country of his no less zealous enemies the Indians.

But it would not do to risk all upon too sudden a change, as it was not certain how long the pursuit would be kept up, nor what direction it would take. That they could possibly track him thus far Ralph did not believe, and the only danger he ran was that of being stumbled upon by a random searcher.

These considerations induced him to pause where he was, and remain quiet, keeping a look-out upon all sides, to see that no unwelcome visitor approached his vicinity. There was a stream of pure water near by, and his abun-dant repast of the night before had driven all thoughts of present hunger from his mind.

Noon came and passed. The fugitive was quite re-freshed, and yet no signs of foes. Strengthened by the hearty food of which he had partaken the night previous, and anxious to avoid any chance capture, he resolved to set out immediately for the western wilderness. There he would be safe, for a time at least, and could give body and mind that rest so much needed.

Passing down to the creek he bent over, and took a hearty drink of the crystal waters. It was refreshing and delightful to his wearied frame, and as it was ques-tionable when he might meet with tolerable water again, he bent over and took a second draught.

" Ugh !"

As the youth was rising to his feet, a deep, guttural voice upon the other side of the stream pronounced a single exclamation; and two men, very similar in physical development, but very unlike in outer characteristics, stood regarding each other dubiously.

The intruder was none other than Ralph's sometime

friend and preserver, Elk's Foot, the Indian prince! Evidently his surprise at the meeting was no less than that of Ralph. Neither had a weapon in hand, and neither seemed fully to comprehend the other's feelings toward him.

"Elk's Foot glad to meet pale-face 'gain," that individual finally remarked, looking around him as much as possible without, however, taking his eyes from the man he addressed.

"I can't say that I am 'specially glad of any such thing," returned Ralph, who was chagrined at the meeting. "You didn't use me especially well when I saw you before."

"Me hunted for you long while," pursued the Indian. "Now me find you, take you back to Sleeping Fawn."

"Guess not," remarked Ralph, who was getting one hand upon the lock of a pistol. "You'll have to be too smart for me if you do."

Before he could produce the weapon, however, the savage had uttered a loud yell, and sprung across the stream. He produced a hatchet at the same moment, but before it could be drawn back into a striking position, Ralph had grasped him, and a fierce struggle ensued.

In bulk and physical power the two combatants were quite equally matched—the Indian being a trifle taller, and not quite so heavily built as his antagonist. The white, however, was much the more supple, and played around the confused Indian in his own manner. The latter, although he had probably never grasped that man whom he could not vanquish, and somewhat surprised by the peculiar movements of the hunter, was no mean antagonist. He defied every effort to throw him to the earth, and at times had his hatchet dangerously free.

But Ralph as steadily foiled every attempt to strike on the Indian's part, and generally gained some slight advantage in turn.

But the contest gave promise of too great duration, and the white resolved upon a bold expedient for ending it. The struggle had occurred upon the bank of the creek, which both had taken care to avoid at first. Now he sprung quickly into the water, drawing the savage after him. The result was what he had anticipated. The tall Indian lost his footing, and with a slight effort Ralph threw him headlong into the stream.

While Elk's Foot was floundering in the disturbed flood, the victor sprung quickly to the shore, and started off through the forest at almost lightning speed. He realized that the Indian's followers were probably near at hand, and discretion under such circumstances would be more to his purpose than headlong rashness.

He was right in suspecting their proximity, for he had scarcely sped fifty yards upon his course when a shout arose, and looking back he saw that a number of Indians had appeared upon the scene of his late struggle with their chief. He had barely time to throw himself behind a tree when two or three guns were discharged, and the balls whistled so closely as to leave no doubt of their fatal effects had he not taken the precaution he did.

Much as he would have delighted to return the shots, he had no time for so doing. Gathering all his strength he bounded away, and though other missiles whistled after and about him, none of them came within dangerous distance.

"Fire away!" he muttered, darting on with unabated speed. "You can't shoot without losing time, and while you are blazing away I'll be running!"

The truth of this reasoning soon became so apparent to the Indians that they desisted from firing, and bent all their energy to the pursuit. Ralph had gained sufficiently during the few moments which had been allowed him, to give him quite a tolerable chance in the race which was to follow. The Indians, however, were never more determined than upon the present occasion, and for miles the race was continued without any apparent advantage to either side. The savages were more scattered, one or two, and Elk's Foot who led the party, being nearer than at the commencement, while others had fallen back, almost out of sight. Ralph had taken a western route, so that he was making ground in the right direction. Still, he preferred to take his time in making his journey, and to do it without observation. Besides, the long-continued exertion was telling upon his worn frame, and he began to feel the need of at least a short respite. His resolve was soon taken. He would endeavour to check the progress of his foes.

His rifle had been slung over his back, but he managed readily to disengage it, and then he looked at the priming as he ran. It was in perfect order, and without any hesitation he wheeled quickly, placed the barrel beside a sapling to insure it from any tremulous motion, and levelled it at Elk's Foot, who was in advance, and quite near.

It really seemed hard to take the life of one who had twice saved his own, and if Ralph had reasoned more upon the matter his noble soul might have refused to sanction the attempt. But he had no time for nice calculations, and with a steady aim he pulled the trigger !

There was a flash—then a report; but the weapon hung fire for a moment. Elk's Foot was unharmed, though one of his followers, at a considerable distance, was stricken down by the bullet.

"So ho!" he thought, turning to continue his flight. "I might have expected as much. My hand is getting so unsteady that I can't even shoot—that doesn't argue well for my getting clear of this yelling tribe. Possibly I can load on a run and not lose ground much. I'll try it."

He had often practised this exercise, and few could handle a rifle more readily than himself, yet he found it a serious task to ram home the bullet without slackening his speed to a great extent. Still, he succeeded, and was withdrawing the ramrod, when it slipped from his hand to the ground. This was an accident of no trifling moment in such a life-and-death race as the present. He was obliged to stop upon the instant and retrace several steps before regaining it. As he did so one of the Indians fired, his bullet cutting close to the young man's head, but producing no injury.

Just as he regained the rod, and was upon the point of resuming his flight, Elk's Foot came to a halt, and hurled his hatchet with great fury. The distance was long, but Ralph only escaped a wound by stepping to one side. At the same time he drew a pistol, and fired at the savage with a deliberate aim.

Long as was the range this shot was more successful than that with the rifle had been. Elk's Foot uttered a cry, and grasped one arm with the hand of the other. Instead of continuing to lead the pursuit as he had done, the son of the chief pointed in advance, and urged on his warriors, exhibiting to them his wounded arm. With fresh cries of vengeance they rushed forward.

Ralph had taken advantage of the slight pause to

prime his loaded rifle, and with a quick movement he brought it to bear upon the dusky pursuers. A sharp detonation bespoke the fall of another brave, and again the fugitve turned to flee. But his shot had in no wise slackened the pursuit. The Indians were determined upon giving him no time to reload, and pressed forward at the top of their speed.

Unfortunately for the fugitive they had passed the region of rolling country which had been so opportune for him upon a previous race, and the landscape spread before them a dreary level. The wood was mainly of gigantic growth, and quite open, so that no opportunity presented for strategy. Any deviation from a direct line would only bring him nearer the savages. The only thing he could do was to press directly onward, and trust to fate to deliver him from pursuit.

But steadily the savages came on, gradually gaining, as it seemed to the fugitive hunter. He, on the contrary, began to feel exhausted, and realise that he must succumb should the chase be prolonged for a great length of time. The manifold hardships through which he had passed had told upon his naturally rugged frame.

Looking back, he saw that quite a dozen Indians were still within sight—odds too great for any single man, no matter how bold and courageous. Possibly he might reduce their number. The only question was that of reloading his rifle. He had also a pistol undischarged, and he did not believe a single firearm among the Indians to be loaded.

Shifting his gun, Ralph poured the powder in, and produced a ball, which he fitted to the muzzle of the bore. Then he attempted to draw the rammer. Just at that moment he was undeceived in regard to the state of his enemies' weapons. A gun was discharged behind him, and the bullet whistled near—so near, indeed, as to strike the lower part of his rifle. He glanced down, to assure himself that the weapon was not seriously injured, then proceeded to ram down the ball.

He turned the piece in order to prime, when a gasp of despair burst from his lips. The savage's bullet had carried away the cover to his rifle-pan ! Here was a loss not to be remedied. His most valuable weapon was ruined. With a hasty exclamation he hurled it from him, and the Indians, divining the cause, set up a shout of triumph.

There is a very venerable adage, saying, " Misfortunes never come singly." However true this may be in every-day life, it was certainly the case with Ralph, at that moment. He had scarcely thrown aside his weapon when he found himself in the midst of a densely-tangled vine. He endeavoured to pause, to save himself, but it was too late. His foot caught, and he was thrown to the earth.

Extricating the unfortunate member, he attempted to use it, but found that his knee had been wrenched, and was useless for the moment. Still he raised himself up-right, and with folded arms and a look of defiance, awaited the arrival of his exulting enemies.

He had not long to wait, for the red-men were only too anxious to secure so dangerous a foe. Without any pause they rushed upon and disarmed, but did not bind him. A stalwart savage took him by either arm, and dragged him to an opening, where they waited for the arrival of Elk's Foot, who was some distance behind.

That individual came on at length, having stopped to bind up his torn and bleeding arm. An expression of savage satisfaction mantled his features on beholding the man who had wounded him, and led the fleetest of his tribe such a prolonged race.

" Pale-face great warrior," he said, with a fiendish intonation. " Him run very fast, but no match for the braves of the Wolf-Slayer. The stag is not more fleet of foot than they, and the eagle flies not longer than they run. But pale-face must go to Wolf-Slayer and Sleeping Fawn ; they would see him again, and see him burn ! "

There was something in the words which sent a deadly thrill to the prisoner's heart, but he made little or no reply, and soon the party declared themselves ready to set out for home. Four were sent to bring in the two that had fallen by Ralph's rifle, while the others took a bee-line for their home, striking through the forest as though by instinct.

CHAPTER X.

A MEETING IN THE FOREST.

IT is very seldom that hope utterly deserts the human heart. However signally reason may have failed to discern any gleaning of promise, that sweet angel will still hover near the heart, giving expectation of good even from the most decided evil.

So it was with Ralph Rilley, as his face was turned once more in the direction of the Indian country, escorted by men whose expressed anticipations were of seeing him burned to death ! It was far from being a comforting or pleasurable thought, and reason showed no manner in which he could avoid the intended fate. There was no possibility of hope from his fellow-men—they would be equally anxious to slay him. He was weaponless, and guarded by a band of zealous savages. The only possible opportunity of escape he had spurned, throwing it aside as involving a living death and perpetual dishonour more to be feared than immediate dissolution.

Altogether the picture was not pleasant, nor one which he cared to contemplate. But it was hard to take his mind from surrounding circumstances. Try as he would the fiery spectacle of a man burning at the stake, to appease the honour of a slighted Indian damsel, would intrude upon his fancy. And when he realised that within a few hours, or days at most, he should in all probability have the pleasure of experiencing that novel *auto da fé*, it must be said, in all candour, that a sickly sensation pervaded his being. He longed for forgetfulness—even regretted that he had not resisted to the last gasp, and induced his savage foes to shoot or tomahawk him before surrendering.

Still would hope come in his calmer moments, and whisper various improbable things to him—that he might escape—that the cause of the murder might have been found out, and that his friends would hasten to seek and save him. These, and many more improbable, but not utterly impossible fancies, passed through his mind as he travelled slowly onward.

The long race had taken up the best portion of the afternoon, and wearied the braves exceedingly. So much so, indeed, that after walking a few miles it was decided to stop for the night. Two expert hunters were sent out to provide game for their supper, and the others busied themselves in building a fire, quizzing the prisoner, and smoking pipes—not those of peace, however.

Within an hour the hunters returned, having been fortunate in securing a fine buck. Here was an unexpected treat, the long race having given every participant a keen appetite, not excepting the prisoner. A dozen broad slices soon were broiling upon the coals, filling the forest with an agreeable odour. The hungry natives did not wait for it to cook, however, but snatched the savoury steak before it was really warmed.

Ralph was requested to help himself, but, hungry as he was, preferred to wait until the meat was tolerably cooked. He came near losing it; the hungry warriors having hastily swallowed their first instalments, and rushed greedily for his. But he was on the watch, and bore it away in advance of the tall warrior whose mouth was expressly prepared for it. Thus the meal passed away, the Indians taking delight in the hearty manner of the prisoner, and conferring together in regard to the extent of his sufferings when the flames should begin their deadly work.

But Ralph was not moved by all this; he would not suffer the pangs of hunger now, that he might suffer less in that dread ordeal. Possibly he might escape, and in that case he should need all his strength.

Soon after the meal was eaten, the satiated warriors began to throw themselves upon the ground to sleep. The sun had sunk low, and twilight was gathering over the forest. The prisoner did not regret this move in the least, for possibly he might sleep, and in unconsciousness lose the fearful spectacle which continually presented itself to his waking vision. It is possible that he might have had other fancies, but if so, they were not really dwelt upon.

The Indians soon completed their preparations for his accommodation. These consisted of two long, slender poles, which were put across his body, and upon either end of which a savage was to sleep. This was not entirely a comfortable arrangement for the prisoner, but evidently quite as much so for him as for those who lay beside him.

A single scout had been sent out, who described a circle around the camp, and finding all in order, returned, and threw himself upon the ground near the fire. In a very short time all seemed to be sleeping soundly.

Ralph felt the need of rest, but his eyes would not close. Thoughts of the fate which must soon be his kept all possibility of drowsiness at bay. Finally he began to think it possible that his most sanguine hopes were to be realised during the night. Surely while his captors were sleeping so soundly, if ever, he ought to be able to leave them.

True, the Indians had undertaken to provide against any possibility of his leaving, but after examining all the circumstances thoroughly, he felt that with prudence and skill he might extricate himself without waking the savages sleeping beside him.

The poles which had been used to confine him were quite pliant, and by gently pressing upward with one foot, he was enabled to withdraw the other. This was one point gained. He was proceeding to extricate the second, moving very carefully, when the savage upon his right side sprung suddenly to his feet and grasped his gun.

Ralph was startled, thinking that his indiscretion had cost his life. But he was immensely relieved when the Indian moved away into the forest. Very soon he returned, uttered a growl of disappointment, and threw himself down to sleep. He noticed the fact of Ralph having withdrawn both feet from beneath the rod which confined them, moved the pole up a foot or so toward the prisoner's body, and threw himself upon it again.

Another tedious waiting followed, until the guard was
sleeping soundly, and then Ralph began to experiment
with a view to regaining his liberty. But he was very
soon satisfied that any movement of his, sufficient to free
his limbs, would awaken one or both of his watchers, and
perhaps insure him immediate death. Still he was willing
to run the risk, since there was everything to gain—
nothing to lose.

Ralph had commenced the work of extrication, and was
progressing very slowly, when a circumstance occurred to
hasten his proceedings. The Indian upon his left gave a
grunt, and rolled away from him, removing his body from
one of the rods, which flew upward with a bound.
Nothing could have been more fortunate for the young
man's purposes than this move. He was at once enabled
to extricate his lower limbs, and the feeling of freedom
which thrilled through his frame was invigorating.

As though an invisible hand was assisting the prisoner
(and who shall say that such was not the case?), the
Indian drew away still further, and the remaining pole
raised itself into the air. Ralph could scarce restrain his
joy at such signal and unwitting assistance. He had
scarcely command enough of his nervous system to refrain
from springing to his feet and bounding away through
the forest. But he mastered the joyful emotions, and
very carefully and slowly crawled away from the fatal
vicinity.

A moment more and he would be free. Was it to be ?
Carefully he stole away, inch by inch almost, listening,
longing, hoping for the boon which hung by a single
thread. Just at the instant when he would have broken
away from the scene, he heard a savage moving. Was he
to be discovered? At that time he stood beside a small

tree, the branches of which hung within reaching distance of the ground.

Almost without any settled purpose he swung himself into the branches, and noiselessly gained a respectable distance from the ground. Here he paused to notice the movements within the Indian camp.

As he had feared, his absence became known in a moment, and the camp was in an uproar. Very silently the Indians spread into the forest, gliding along like so many spectres. Ralph knew his chance would have been less than nothing had he attempted flight. In a few moments all the Indians had dispersed, leaving him alone.

Noticing the direction taken by his enemies, he slid to the ground, and flitted off into the woods, using excessive caution. Having proceeded but a few rods, he again mounted into a friendly tree whose branches would afford him certain security as long as darkness remained. His purpose, however, was to rest there for an hour or more until the savages should give up the search, then to take to his feet again. Ere long, one by one, the Indians came in. He could see the dull camp-fire from his perch, and counted their numbers, until at length all were in, the last being Elk's Foot. At once a council was held. Then was the moment to fly, since the council would surely end in arrangements for a thorough search of the forest as soon as the light permitted. Slipping down from his leafy covert, Ralph once more trod the forest mazes—a hunted man.

When once clear of the dangerous vicinity it was but natural that he should begin to reflect upon what lay before him. Where to go, and what to do? Alone and weaponless, hunted and doomed both by his fellow whites and the Indians, his case was desperate indeed.

As he could not live in the forest without weapons, or some method of procuring food, his first impulse was to return to Forest Valley, and seek for a new supply. But this would be a most dangerous experiment, since his late appearance there had, no doubt, put those who sought his life doubly upon their guard. Extensive as had been his border and forest experience, he knew of no retreat where he might safely hide from his numerous enemies. His only safety was in putting such a distance between himself and them as would render futile all their attempts against him.

As his present course was toward the east, the very reverse of the direction he wished to take, he only continued it for such time as seemed sufficient to carry him beyond the savages' reach. Then he turned his steps to the south-east, heading for Forest Valley. Not that he really intended to revisit the place, but an irresistible influence drew him thence.

He travelled some miles in the new direction, and then stopped. He was uncertain as to the exact distance he might have travelled, and, as morning already was paling the eastern stars, he resolved to wait until its beams should reveal his whereabouts. He was far from feeling anxious for further adventures, if they could possibly be avoided.

Daylight came at length, and Ralph soon satisfied himself as to his whereabouts. He was within ten miles of Forest Valley, in a region he had frequently visited.

He was undecided which of two plans to pursue. Probably he could remain where he was till late in the day, and stand comparatively small chances of being discovered. Then he could shape his course toward Forest Valley, and seek an interview with his brother during the coming night. He could thus procure a rifle, and make another attempt to gain an asylum in the western wilderness. Failing of this, he must take to the forest, and endeavour to obtain a living from such berries and roots as he could find.

Seeking a refuge as well sheltered from the casual passer as might be readily found, the young man threw himself upon the ground, and was soon asleep. So deeply exhausted was he by the past nights of unrest, that it was nearly noon before he awoke.

He would have sprung to his feet at once on seeing how high the sun had mounted, but recollecting the circumstances which surrounded him, used due caution before making any move. He was scanning the region before and around him, when the sound of footsteps at a little distance in his rear startled him. Plainly he could hear them, slow and stealthy. Almost afraid to look around the broad trunk which sheltered him, Ralph prepared for a struggle, and waited till the intruder should come.

But the footsteps, instead of drawing nearer, seemed to retreat. Cautiously peering around the tree, Ralph saw that the form was indeed moving away—and he saw something else, too. The intruder was a woman! Not only that, but he had recognised the clothing, and sprung to his feet, with a quick and joyous exclamation :—

" My God, I thank thee ?"

The woman heard the movements, and uttered a low cry of terror, for she had supposed no human being was near her. But, when she heard the young man's devout exclamation, she stopped, and turned about with an eager trembling expression.

" Ralph, my dear Ralph, is it really you ?" she asked,

moving toward him and sinking upon the strong arm which was extended to her support. "Thank heaven, I have found a friend at last!"

"Yes, my beloved girl, it is none other," he said, gazing down into the pale and sorrow-marked features. "But I am scarcely worth the considering as a friend. I am only an outlaw, hunted and doomed!"

"What do you mean?" she demanded. "You— Ralph—an outlaw? I do not comprehend!"

"It is a fact," he replied; "I am charged with having killed your father, and am hunted like a wolf, to be hung at the first tree."

"Ralph—Ralph! can this be possible? Can men be so blind and cruel? And you above all others!" She bowed her head on his shoulder, and wept convulsively for a while. When her grief had somewhat subsided, he drew her to a seat beside a fallen tree, and related in succinct terms the occurrences of the past ten days. And then he, in turn, listened to an account of what had befallen the maiden during the same eventful period.

CHAPTER XI.

NOT YET.

FOR some time the joyful couple sat in silence. Both felt more fully than they could express in words the joys of that reunion. The weary and worn Nancy, after all her wanderings, had found the one whom of all others she felt to be most capable of protecting her, and encircled by his strong arm she forgot all the dangers of the past— those terrible sorrows and trials which had embittered her young life were swallowed up in the present safety and happiness.

Ralph, if he did not feel equally safe and assured in regard to their present situation, was equally happy—if possible, even more so. The dark cloud which had hung over his name for so many weary days—which had sub-jected him to persecution—driven him from the presence of his fellow-men to wander like a haunted spirit, driven from place to place with no rest, no sympathy, no mercy —hunted and doomed, all this seemed removed afar from him. He could return once more to home and friends, proud and happy to assert his entire innocence, bringing with him the lost loved one, with convincing testimony to reinstate him in all the dignity of his former unsullied manhood.

Surely this was sufficient cause for happiness and self-congratulation. His heart rose and swelled as he con-templated so great a consummation. No more would he think of self-exile in the lonely wilds of the unknown forests ; no more start and flee from every sound, or every appearance of his brother man.

Again he pressed the maiden to his breast, murmuring as he did so :—

" Thank God, I shall be free from this terrible taint of suspicion once more. I shall owe my whole life to you, dearest love. I can only hope to prove my sincerity by a life of devotion."

" I am glad of that, Ralph, right glad," was the earnest reply, " for I shall need your protection. You know that I am alone in the world—all alone in the great, wide, strange world, Ralph ; and I shall sadly need some one who is my friend indeed to keep me from danger and trouble in the future."

" Our life shall be very happy, Nancy, for we will live only for each other. I have loved you long and intensely, but up to the present moment never realised how Providence had linked our destinies together. It must be that a power higher and greater than any here below rules and executes judgment upon earth."

"No doubt of it, Ralph; we see evidences of its existence about us every day."

The young man mused a moment, and then in a meditative mood he pursued :—

"I have doubted it at times, I will confess. When I could not see the wisdom or purpose which lay hidden behind some dark design, I have felt that chance—or a strange mixture of good and evil—ruled in our earthly affairs. And yet we cannot see the end of His purposes —we only see the dark side of the present to inspire our doubts, while the brighter side, which should encourage our faith, is too often overlooked in the pleasures of the moment."

Then recollecting himself, he added :—

"One would almost think I were studying to be a preacher. But I happened to feel just so, and could not help speaking out. You have not yet told me who the murderer was."

"Spare me that!" Nancy moaned, with an almost frightened air. "I really cannot bear to recall that dark scene till I am forced to do so. When called upon to relate the dark adventures of that fearful night, I will do it in full; but till that time comes the theme is too painful."

"Pardon me, Nancy, I was thoughtless. Now, if you feel quite rested, we will resume our way, for many a danger may still intervene between us and home."

"I know it well, Ralph. And I fear we shall find it very difficult to elude the Indians. No doubt they are searching for me, and between the two bands it will be wonderful good luck if we get safe to Forest Valley. Oh, I cannot, cannot go back again to their dreadful haunts! I would rather die!"

" Let us hope for the best, dearest. I am well used to these forests, and if they do not get a glimpse of us, I have no doubt we can elude them, even if they should get upon our trail."

They rose to go, Ralph supporting the weary form of the dear girl as they moved through a mass of bushes and undergrowth, where their progress was very slow and difficult. At every step Nancy took her garments caught and tore.

" Oh, how provoking!" she exclaimed, as her dress caught upon a small unseen thorn-bush, from which it was no easy task to extricate it.

Stepping back to loosen the grasp of the sharp spurs, something in the forest beyond caught her attention, and with a low cry of horror and despair she sunk low among the bushes.

Ralph looked quickly up for the cause of her alarm, and his own emotions were none of the pleasantest on beholding a stealthy Indian gliding through the forest, scarcely a hundred yards away! For a single moment he stood spell-bound, then threw himself upon the ground beside Nancy. Possibly the savage had not espied them, and would pass without being aware of their presence. He had certainly manifested no knowledge of their proximity, and the bushes were sufficiently high to shelter them from sight, unless he came very near. In any case Ralph felt that they could do no better. To flee or fight —the only resorts which suggested themselves—was impossible.

" We are lost, lost !" groaned Nancy, whose fond visions of rest and safety were all scattered in a moment.

" 'Sh !" whispered Ralph. " He may not see us. If we are careful not to attract his attention it is hardly probable that he will take the pains to pass through this bramble. Do you lie close while I push up through these briers and see what direction he takes."

Nancy complied implicitly, and Ralph, by cautiously raising his head, was soon enabled to see the ground where the Indian had stood. As he expected, the savage was not there ; neither was he at any point between. Satisfied that he had moved away in some other direction, Ralph, strangely enough, forgot a portion of his habitual cunning, and raised his head still higher, in the hope of seeing the red man. Naturally he was anxious to know which way his foe had gone, so as to guard against a future encounter.

But, as the event proved, the Indian was not far away, and had really outwitted the white. As the latter raised his head a second time, he observed a jet of flame and smoke from a small tree at some distance, a bullet whistled through his clothing, cutting a lock of hair from his uncovered head in its passage, and buried itself in the ground beside him.

Many years in the forest had taught Ralph Rilley that apparently the most reckless course often proved wisest in the result. Acting upon this idea, the young man no sooner felt the passage of the bullet than he sprung to his feet, and dashed, with a yell, toward the tree containing the savage. All unarmed as he was, the act partook of the most utter rashness, yet it produced the very result he hoped for.

The Indian was not prepared for any such movement.

Never doubting that his bullet would end the life of a foe to his race, he was peering anxiously forward to note the result, when he was surprised to behold an athletic form bound through the bushes, and dash in the direction of his perch. Recoiling in surprise, he lost his balance and tumbled to the ground. Gathering himself up, he flew into the forest with bounds like those of a frightened deer.

Ralph had no intention of pursuing. He was prepared for nothing of the kind. Merely satisfying himself that the savage would not look around for some moments, he sprung back to the place where he had left Nancy. The maiden still crouched upon the ground, trembling in mortal terror. She could not comprehend the rash movements of her lover; it seemed to her that he was only rushing upon certain death.

"Come!" he said, raising her in his arms, and bounding through the bramble. "We must make an effort to fly. It is our only chance now—heaven only knows if we shall be successful!"

He placed her upon the ground, after passing the obstructions in which they had been involved, and then both sped forward, striking toward another copse of bushes at some distance, which seemed to give promise of a more secure shelter. Nancy exerted herself to the utmost, though at heart she had very little hope of escaping. But the horrors of her late imprisonment loomed up before her imagination like a black cloud, and she dreaded death less than a hopeless return to its horrors. Even Ralph was surprised at the zeal with which she ran, keeping close beside him without retarding his own movements in the least.

Rapidly the distance was passed—they had almost reached the copse. Were they to gain it, and temporary shelter ? A moment of time, and they would be within its friendly bosom. Onward—if another rod can be passed they will be concealed from the eyes of savage faces, for the growth is dense, so dense, that at their present distance they cannot see beyond the green barrier. How hope rises, but rises only to be blighted !

A loud, savage yell from far behind rings out upon the air, and the half-uttered exclamation of joy gives place to a groan of despair.

"We are lost, Ralph !" gasped Nancy, grasping his arm.

"Not yet !" stoutly repeated the young ranger, seizing her in turn, and making his way through the bushy veil. "We won't give up till the last moment, under any circumstances."

With an experienced eye he took in at a single glance the peculiarities of their situation.

A little thread of water, scarcely sufficient to form a stream, ran along through the forest, its banks being heavily fringed with bushes for some distance up and down from the spot where they stood. Its general course was diagonal to that taken by the lovers, so that by bending a little to the south-west they could follow down its banks. This Nancy seemed to regard as a foregone conclusion, and turned at once in that direction. But Ralph quickly called her back.

"This way, love," he said, pointing in the other direction.

Then as he grasped her hand and hurried on, he added, in a low tone :—

"They will look down-stream for us. Our only hope lies in slipping into the bushes, and waiting until we can glide away in some other direction without attracting their notice.   If we can do this, all may yet turn out right."

At the same moment the foremost Indian reached the place where they had disappeared from his sight, and they paused opposite a cluster of weeds and bushes more dense than any they had passed.   By good fortune they had taken shelter there a moment before the Indian burst through the bushes, and stood gazing perplexed in either direction.

As they had hoped, he bent his course rapidly down stream, keeping his gun in readiness for instant use, and peering into every place which might afford shelter to those he sought.

But if the movements of the leading savage gave com fort and hope to the hidden ones, those of his followers did not.   Word was at once passed that the fugitives were missing, and the savages divided into groups, part going down the stream, and as many coming in the direc tion of the lovers.

It was certainly too late now to think of any further flight.   They had done all that could be done, and re- signing themselves to the fate that seemed inevitable, they awaited the result of the Indians' search.   Yet, even with the gloom of despair settling over them, came a ray of hope to the soul of Ralph.   Those he must encounter were not those from whom he had previously escaped. No doubt these would recognise and bear him back to their village as a great prize ; but he would still have some time for planning, and very possible it seemed that his lucky star might again be in the ascendant.

These reasonings were founded upon the supposition that the Indians would discover and take him captive, This supposition proved perfectly correct.

A dusky Indian parted the bushes, glanced in, gave a triumphant grunt, and beckoned his companions forward. Two of them came, and after gloating over the helpless condition of their prisoners, the first comer presented his gun, saying, in tolerable English :—

"Come out, pale-faces. Me take you home. You chil'en—git lost in big woods !"

A grunt of satisfaction, quite as near a laugh as was allowable with the dignity of a full-fledged warrior, broke from the other savages at this witticism; after which they, too, presented their weapons, and called upon the whites to come forth.

Knowing that resistance or non-compliance would not only be useless, but quite likely to provoke dangerous consequences from the Indians, they complied, and were exultingly seized by their captors, who raised a note of recall to their searching brethren. Very soon a dozen zealous savages had gathered about the party. They were in raptures over the result of their search, for they had not only secured the pale maiden of whom they were in pursuit, but the young man whom their brothers were looking for. As in all matters of like moment, guards were placed over the prisoners, while a council was held. The only question which arose was, whether to search for the other party, or repair at once to their village.

The latter counsel prevailed. They would take the captives home with them, and when Elk's Foot and his companions returned, weary and crestfallen, they would rejoice and boast over them, producing the two captives which they had taken, while the son of a chief searched in vain.

Having reached this conclusion, six men were deployed

to scour for game, and look for any signs of their companions. The remainder, escorting the prisoners, moved in a body, travelling rapidly till near sunset, when they stopped upon the margin of a large natural pond, which had been appointed as a place of rendezvous.

No sooner had they halted than Ralph and his companion were bound, and firmly lashed to stout saplings. At first, the thoughts of an informal *auto da fě* were very naturally uppermost; but these were speedily dissipated by the movements of the Indians. Having secured their captives, fishing-tackle of every description was produced, and with spear and hook, the finny inhabitants of the pond were assailed. The greedy savages waited not for culinary process or ceremony. Every luckless fish which fell into their power was stripped of the most unpalatable portions, sliced up, and swallowed with a gusto which shocked the more civilized witnesses.

At length one, more considerate or with less appetite than his fellows, brought a small slice to each of the prisoners, after which he resumed his seat in the circle, and ate till the last morsel had disappeared.

Having disposed of their food, the savages relaxed the ropes which held the prisoners sufficiently to allow of their lying down, then threw themselves upon the bare earth, and silence reigned over the vast forest.

CHAPTER XII.

SOMETHING OR NOTHING.

RALPH waited till satisfied that all the Indians were sleeping soundly, when he began to work out the possibility of escape, but he soon found that any such effort would be vain. The cords which confined him were of deerskin, well worn, so that the knots could be tied in the securest manner. This the Indians had done to perfection, and after a score of fruitless endeavours to loosen hand or foot, Ralph composed himself to get such sleep as was possible, cautioning his companion to adopt the same policy.

Weary and worn as they were, both of them slept very soon, despite the fearful fate which seemed hanging over them. Sleeping visions came to them, certainly, some bringing hope and others winged with despair, but all in all, the rest they obtained was very beneficial.

Before midnight they were aroused, and, upon gaining their feet, found that all their ropes had been cast off save those upon their hands, and the Indians stood around, prepared to resume their journey. With weary limbs and aching hearts the prisoners set forth, wending their way, hour in and hour out, through the forest, stumbling over obstacles without number, meeting with varied detentions, but never pausing till the full light of day flooded the forest, awakening the songs of gladness from thousands of happy-hearted, feathered warblers.

Here they paused for a short rest; but only a few moments were they allowed the pleasure of reposing their wearied frames, ere they were dragged on again, by their zealous and exulting captors. Ralph did not care for himself—he could endure the severest trials which his Indian guards might see fit to impose. But when he considered that Nancy was subjected to the same rigorous treatment, obliged to perform the same long, wearying marches, his heart swelled with indignation, and he longed to vent a just retribution upon the inhuman wretches.

2

Slowly the day wore away. Hungry, weary, and scarce able to stand, the heroic Nancy toiled along, almost ready to stop and meet grim death itself, rather than drag her sinking frame further toward a fate—she knew not how fearful it might be—she shuddered and sickened at the very thought. Only the occasional words which Ralph found opportunity to utter cheered her desponding heart. So long as he hoped, she felt it wrong to quite give way to despair.

Just before dusk they entered the Indian town again. A gloom, as of death, fell over the maiden's spirits—if gloom could be said to cast a shadow over despair. Up to this moment a faint thought had haunted her mind that they might escape or be rescued before reaching the village. But now even this undefined hope fled.

Ralph noticed her mood, and managing to slip near her side, he muttered :—

"We shall have all the night to get away in—what more could we ask?"

"You no say anyfing!" shouted one of the Indians, brandishing a hatchet, as he sprung toward Ralph. "You come wid me!"

He grasped the prisoner by the arm, and dragged him to the other side of the party. Then, assuming an air of grandeur and importance, the braves stalked forward, paying no attention to the rushing squaws and young Indians, who crowded about to see the prisoners, and clamoured for their instant torture.

Presently the old chief, Wolf-Slayer, appeared. The entire procession stopped at his approach, and waited in silence for his will to be made known. The old hunter ran his eyes over the group. They lighted up perceptibly when he saw the pale, pain-marked features of Nancy

Andrews, and a grunt of satisfaction escaped his lips. But when he saw Ralph, and especially when he noticed the look of coolness and daring upon the young hunter's face, the brows of the old Indian contracted, and he turned fiercely upon his heel.

Calling one of the warriors to his side, the two conversed several moments, earnestly.

Having satisfied his feelings, the old chief hurried away, and the party was not long in gaining the midst of the town. Here they scarcely paused, half-a-dozen of the savages leading Ralph away, while as many took another direction with Nancy. The young man endeavoured to follow her with his eyes, but in this he was unsuccessful, and very soon he realised that they were separated again, perhaps for ever.

The young man was conducted again to the strong cabin he had occupied upon his former sojourn. There was an unpleasant look of familiarity about it, everything appearing as it had done when he was placed there before, save that ample precautions had been taken to prevent his escape by the same method.

Very soon, too, he discovered that he was to be more closely guarded than formerly. Two fresh braves, whom he had not seen before, were conducted to the hut very strict orders given them in the jargon of their people. Knowing that nothing could be accomplished at present, Ralph composed himself to sleep, and for some hours was quite oblivious to all that passed in the cabin.

It was dark when he awoke, so dark that for some minutes he was unable to make out the presence of his gloomy hued guards. At length, a cat-like movement gave him a clue, and he was enabled to trace the movement of a dusky form across the cabin, and back again to his side. He noticed that the savage moved about uneasily, as though struggling between duty and inclination.

Presently he bent over the recumbent form of his companion, and they changed places, the relieved guard setting his gun carelessly against the wall, and throwing himself beside it upon the floor. The new sentinel bent over and satisfied himself that the prisoner was sleeping, then walked once or twice across the cabin, before taking up his station. Ralph had noticed every disposition and movement as perfectly as the very uncertain light would permit, and his heart began to swell with hope once more.

It was a desperate move, certainly, but the prize—freedom for himself and Nancy—justified any reasonable risk, and he began to consider how he should gain the end he sought. The gun of the sleeping guard stood almost within his reach. The other sentry was careless, and supposed his charge fast locked in slumber. So much was to his advantage. To offset—his arms were bound behind his back, and all his efforts thus far had failed to loosen the cords. True, there was considerable freedom to his hands, but the knots were most secure.

Finally a thought struck him. He had heard of men crawling backward through their arms, with hands tied as were his own. He had even attempted it himself; but, thus far, had never succeeded. There was sufficient play to his arms; possibly he might succeed in the gymnastic operation, and do it without any noise. Both conditions were essential to success.

Placing his hands flat upon the earth, Ralph drew himself up at a moment when he was not observed, and found that the attempt was likely to prove successful. The very slight noise he made drew the attention of the guard, who hastened toward him. But before his eyes could pierce the gloom the prisoner had resumed his motionless posture, only moving his limbs and groaning heavily.

The guard watched him for some moments, then turned and slowly paced the narrow apartment again, keeping his eyes upon the suspicious form. And yet, under all this scrutiny, Ralph slipped his hands over his feet, and found those useful members in front of him, where he could proceed to liberate them with his teeth.

Even this was no trifling task. The knots had been drawn very tight by his repeated straining upon them, and in the darkness he could not tell when his efforts were rightly directed. But perseverance and determination finally triumphed, and one of his hands was freed. A thrill of joy passed over his frame as this consummation was reached, and he moved very cautiously along the hard-trodden ground several inches before attempting to cast off the cord.

He had just thrown aside the ligature, when a sudden impulse seized the guard, and, running to the spot, he bent over the prisoner. The operation brought his face so close to that of Ralph that the latter could see the gleaming of his eyes, and notice the look of curiosity which mantled his features.

In an instant the captive's resolution was taken, but before it could be carried out he faltered momentarily. It seemed repugnant to his better feelings to act thus treacherously. Only for a moment did he hesitate. The thought of Nancy, of his own doom, of the terrible tragedy at Forest Valley, decided him again.

With a quick spring he half gained his feet, at the same time grasping the Indian's throat with both hands, and hurling him to the ground. Of course, the savage was utterly unprepared for any such movement as this, and before he realised what strange chance had befallen him, found himself prone upon the earth, with a vice-like grasp upon his throat. The Indian made a desperate effort to free himself, but his attempts were perfectly useless so far as regaining his own freedom was concerned. The bulkier white weighed him down like the phantom of some horrible nightmare. The only result to be feared was the awakening of the sleeping guard, who began to move uneasily.

Not a moment's time was to be lost. Ralph steadily tightened his grasp, hoping to force the one beneath him into a lasting quietude before the other should rouse up. But that was not to be. The sleeper opened his eyes, and taking in by intuition the state of affairs, sprung to his feet, with a loud yell.

One less cool and quick-thoughted than Ralph would have been lost at once. Nothing but the promptest action saved his life for a moment. Relaxing his grasp upon the one he held, the young hunter sprung toward the gun, which still leaned against the wall. The owner made a similar move at the same moment, but found himself staggering away from the effect of a stunning blow delivered by the young ranger. Before he could recover himself the latter had possession of the weapon, and was giving a quieting stroke to the second savage, who had made a bootless attempt to rise from the ground.

The contest was now between man and man, the white having the advantage of being armed. The other, however, was making vigorous use of his lungs, and in a very short time would bring down the whole body of Indians to his assistance. Hither and thither the red man sped, avoiding two or three heavy blows which the white aimed at him, and continuing to make night hideous with his cries.

Of course, such a contest must end, sooner or later; and, after several futile efforts, Ralph succeeded in bringing down the gun-stock upon the head of his late guard. Having thus disposed of his attendant foes, he sprung to the door, and undid such of the fastenings as he could find. At the same time a tramping and rush without gave him warning that other Indians were at hand.

Scarcely, indeed, had he reached the door, ere it was burst open, and two Indians rushed into the gloomy hut. Ralph had stepped slightly to one side, and the two passed without observing him. A third paused in the doorway, seeming anxious to penetrate the mystery before advancing further. Possibly his doubts may have been dispelled, certainly his consciousness was, by a blow from the gun which the white still held clubbed.

The Indians heard the sound, perceived that they had been outwitted, and with howls of vengeance sprung to the door. One of their number lay prone with a shattered head, but the bold hunter had gone. Others were on the way, and quickly the news spread that the white prisoner had escaped.

Although dismay seized the bravest at this announcement, they betrayed commendable zeal, rushing into the forest in all directions, and keeping up a steady search for hours—it need hardly be said without success. At length, weary and disheartened, they returned to sleep for a short time, and renew the search again upon the morrow.

Meanwhile, where was the man who had thus, by good fortune more than any merit of his own, escaped the clutches of his bloody-minded enemies, and thrown the Indian town in such a state of excitement?

Knowing that not a moment was to be lost if he would gain the sheltering forest, Ralph, on reaching the open air, bounded away between two huts, and soon found himself safe in the wooded solitudes. The savages were but just spreading the alarm, so that he had plenty of time to adopt any course of action which might seem most proper. That he could easily secure his own freedom he had no doubts. Yet, what did personal liberty avail him, if the maiden whom he loved, and who held the secret of that terrible mystery, remained behind? Honour, duty, necessity, all demanded that she should be released, or he remain to share her fate.

Finding a tree which he could readily climb, Ralph perched himself among its branches, and assumed an easy position. Then he bent his ear toward the town and listened intently.

" That is right," he mused. " They are going to look for me in this darkness, when they needn't think o' such a thing as finding me. By and by they'll give it up, and then go about it again in the morning. While they are sleeping I will attend to the balance of my work. If I do not succeed, it shall not be my fault."

Keeping perfectly quiet while the search progressed under and about him, the daring hunter waited till all was again silent. Then slipping to the ground he crawled carefully back toward the village, listening as he went for any movements among the inhabitants. To find the whereabouts of Nancy, and rescue her, if possible, was now his object.

Soon he reached the rear of a cabin, the nearest of a group which he felt sure contained Nancy. All was dark and silent about it—no signs of life were there.

The second cabin contained the remains of a smouldering fire, which lighted it up sufficiently to assure him of the character of its inmates. Passing thence by two other miserable structures, which seemed upon the point of falling down merely from the force of gravitation, he paused in the rear of another, built much more strongly and in every way larger and superior to any he had yet seen. Instantly the feeling came over him that he gazed upon the prison of Nancy Andrews. To confirm or dispel his suspicion was first to be attempted.

CHAPTER XIII.

A DISCOVERY.

CLOSE to the walls of the Indian dwelling stood Ralph, peering, listening, hoping. There were no sounds to be heard within, no light that he had yet discovered, nor any signs of living beings. But the walls were firmly built, the door, which was strong, was closed and fastened upon the inside. Here were two additional reasons for supposing that the place was a prison.

With some difficulty he found a narrow aperture near the ground, and applying his eye to this he peered into the darksome recesses beyond. For some time he was unable to distinguish anything, and was upon the point of moving away, when a glow, as from a single coal, met his eye. Steadily he watched, and soon after another appeared, revealing the outlines of a savage, stirring the embers of an almost extinct fire.

Having collected the few coals which remained, the Indian added some light brushwood, and soon a cheerful glow pervaded the apartment. The savage then walked away, and bent over a couch of skins, upon which appeared a prostrate form. Apparently satisfied at what he saw, the brave gave a grunt, and turned back to the fire, raising and carefully examining a gun standing in one corner.

Ralph was now satisfied that he had discovered the whereabouts of Nancy, but how should he acquaint her with his presence ?   How could her rescue be effected?

Turning to seek some mode of communication, he glanced at the eastern horizon.   To his surprise, the first faint tinges of dawn were perceptible along the sky.   It was certainly too late to effect anything that night—he would only seek to inform her of his freedom and presence, to inspire her with hope.

Continued search finally revealed a small aperture quite near where her head must lie, and applying his lips to this he gently breathed :—

" Nancy !"

Waiting a moment, he fancied there was a slight movement within, and willing to run all risks, he repeated the name a trifle more distinctly than before.   For a moment he was left in doubt, then a gentle voice, which he would have recognised anywhere, whispered :—

" Ralph !"

" I am here, Nancy ; I am free !" he whispered.   " But it is almost morning, I cannot get you away to-night. Can you remain here safely another day ?"

" I think so."

" Then make the effort, and you shall be released with the coming of night again.   I must go now—the safety of both of us depends upon it.   Use any excuse to gain time, and do not sleep till I come to you."

The maiden gave him some hints, informing him that the cabin in which she was confined was the dwelling of Wolf-Slayer and his family ; that one guard was kept over her constantly, and all the rigour that an apparent friendship and regard could devise thrown about her movements. She also described to him the construction of the building, and the only probable way of gaining the interior.

Ralph listened attentively, and then bade her a brief farewell. He was not a moment too soon. Zealous Indians were upon the look-out, and in five minutes after he left the place, they were astir, preparing for a thorough pursuit of the escaped prisoner. Of course, they had little suspicion that the individual in question was so near them.

Knowing that the pursuit would be carried on chiefly toward Forest Valley, Ralph bent his steps into the forest in an opposite direction. This course, although it might bring him in conjunction with other bodies of savages, would take him away from the vicinity of his most deadly enemies. And yet he would be in a situation to return upon the following night, and redeem the promise given his beloved.

He walked a long distance before daylight began to reveal the outlines of the forest about him; so far, indeed, that he began to look around for some secluded spot in which to pass the long hours before darkness would again cover the earth.

He found it at length ; a broad, massive pile of rocks, pierced with many openings, where men might have been concealed from boyhood with very little danger of discovery. Into one of these caverns Ralph crawled, but drew back as a huge rattlesnake sounded its note of alarm and slowly withdrew. The suspicion that he might be going into a large den of the vipers was far from pleasant.

Observation, however, convinced him that the veteran

he had disturbed was sole occupant ; so after a little hesitation he entered the recess, placed a stone in the hole
through which the reptile had disappeared, and proceded
to take possession. A natural projection in one corner
afforded him a comfortable seat, and here he sat for some
time, planning and reflecting upon the strange circumstances which had befallen him for the past two days.

Noon came and passed. Ralph felt satisfied that if
the Indians had intended to make any search in his
direction they would have reached the lodge long before.
Reasoning thus, he sallied out, and sought for such roots
and herbs as would serve to satisfy his hunger. It was
no pleasant task, but he could assuage the demands of
nature in no other way. True the gun he had brought
from the Indian town was loaded, and he might have
shot something with the single bullet it contained. But
in that case he would have been almost weaponless, and
who could say how valuable a bullet might prove to him
in the proposed enterprise of the coming night.

Having satisfied his inner man as far as possible, Ralph
returned to his cave, and sitting down upon the stone he
had formerly occupied, mused upon his chances of success
till he fell asleep.

When he awoke he perceived that the time for action
was near. The sun was already low behind the distant
hills, and by the time he could reach the scene of operations it would be quite dark enough for his purpose.
Shaking more priming into the pan of his piece, and
shutting it very carefully, he turned his face in the
proper direction.

It was quite dark before Ralph reached the vicinity of
the Indian town. As there was no moon during the
early part of the night, he could have no more oppor-

time time for carrying out his purpose, if other things should prove favourable.

His mind was somewhat troubled, as he neared the place, to observe that a crowd was gathered very near the building he wished to enter, engaged in some mysterious rite, the nature of which he did not comprehend. He was filled with the liveliest fears for a time; but on reaching the vicinity, which the darkness enabled him to do without observation, he saw that the performance boded no ill to Nancy.

The idea naturally arose—could he not rescue her while the attention of the Indians was directed in another channel? The supposition was speedily negatived when he crept beneath the walls of the building, and peered in upon the inmates. Nancy was there, pale and sorrowing. With her was the Indian princess whose love Ralph had rejected, and a sentinel. The latter, with a gun in hand, divided his attention between the ceremony in front, and the prisoner beside him.

So much Ralph saw at a glance, and then he glided away like a shadow. He had partially formed a plan in his own mind, which, though bold and dangerous, promised success.

The dwelling of Wolf-Slayer had been constructed after civilized models, in so far that it had one door and a window—the latter being a square hole cut through the wall, and closed in winter by replacing the original logs. In the present case this window was open, affording possible ingress to the sleeping apartment of Wolf-Slayer; that individual having divided his somewhat extensive domicile into three rooms upon the ground by partitions of poles.

Into the apartment reserved for Wolf-Slayer's especial

use, Ralph quietly made his way, concealing himself beneath a pile of robes and furs. Of course, he had chosen a position to observe everything passing in the outer or main apartment.

More than an hour elapsed before the pow-wow without ceased, and then the crowd gradually began to disperse. Wolf-Slayer entered his dwelling, clothed in robes of state, and ordered the princess to retire, which she did, with a sullen frown. Nancy was then ordered to her couch of skins, and the guard instructed to make sure that she did not stir therefrom during the night. Then the surly chief entered his own apartment, fastened down the bearskin which served as a door, threw aside his royal robes, and stretched himself upon the couch.

Silence soon reigned within and around the building, and Ralph realised that the most opportune moments for getting away from the place were passing. Still he did not dare move as yet, for he had no proof that Wolf-Slayer or Sleeping Fawn had yet succumbed to the drowsy god. He had no hopes now save in perfect success; failure would certainly bring death to both himself and her he sought to save.

Anxiously he watched the movements of the sentinel without, wishing that he might prove careless or indifferent. His wishes were met. Soon the watcher placed his gun in a corner, and busied himself in pacing the room, keeping an eye upon the form of Nancy, to make sure that she did not transgress the commands of Wolf-Slayer.

At length came the sounds for which Ralph had listened so long. The chief was asleep, and snoring soundly. So far as he was concerned there was now comparatively nothing to fear. The partition between the waiting white and the room of Sleeping Fawn was quite thin, and by listening closely he could hear her steady breathing between the sonorous blasts of her father. She, too, was insensible to all about her. There remained but the sentinel to dispose of.

This was no ordinary task. Of course, the slightest noise would defeat the entire plan. Caution, patience, daring, were required in extraordinary degrees.

A thought struck Ralph. Carefully emerging from his hiding-place, he threw Wolf-Slayer's royal robe over his shoulders, and slipped into the apartment which contained the subject of his schemes. The sentinel's back was toward him at the moment, and slipping into a dark corner, beside the heavy fireplace, he waited an opportune moment for the carrying out of his plan. While thus waiting, his hand touched something cold and hard. It was a hatchet—the very thing he needed for the fatal but necessary blow. Carefully disengaging it, he waited for the moment.

It was very dark in the apartment now; Ralph could scarcely discern the form of his victim. The latter seemed to notice the fact, and hastened to replenish the fire, which was the only means of light. The time was at hand. As he bent over, his head was within reach of Ralph's arm. Silently the weapon whirled through the air, and almost as silently the Indian pitched forward upon his face.

The hunter could not bear the idea of a deliberate murder, and had struck but a stunning blow; yet so effectually had it been given that there seemed no prospect of the savage raising an immediate alarm. Ralph proceeded to secure the gun and ammunition of the fallen sentry, tied his belt about him, and stocked it in due form with knife and hatchet.

Then, and how his heart beat, he approached the place where Nancy was lying. Death or deliverance was at hand; which was it to be? He found that the maiden was already cognizant of his movements, and rose to her feet at his approach. Her frame trembled violently under the excitement of the moment, and she led the way toward the door, remarking :—

"Come, come. Do not let us lose a moment in this dreadful place!"

Ralph opened the door very cautiously, and succeeded in closing it again, after they had passed through, without any disturbance. They were now in the open air, and all was silent about them. Already they tasted the bliss of freedom.

"We will take the most direct route possible," said he, after they had left the Indian town behind. "If they do not discover our flight till morning, and it is hardly probable that they will make any pursuit before that time, we shall get such a start as ought to take us to Forest Valley in advance of them."

"Have no fear for me," urged Nancy. "I am rested and strong. I could travel home without making any pause, if it were necessary. Anything to escape these dreadful savages!"

Steadily onward through the long night hours they pushed their way, keeping a bee-line toward home, so nearly as it was possible to travel. When the stars faded away, and daylight came, they were far on their way, and still no sign of pursuit. Hope rose in their bosoms. Fortune seemed to have selected them as the special recipients of her favours.

Having plenty of ammunition, Ralph shot some game, and making a little fire in a secluded spot, they cooked a palatable breakfast. This disposed of, with a relish and heartfelt thanks for their safety thus far, they paused for a short time to rest before again resuming their tedious journey.

CHAPTER XIV.
SATISFIED.

In a short time the two set forward again, and although the journey before them was long, it was cheerfully undertaken. Surely, each of them had sufficient cause for thankfulness. That their lives had been spared through so many dangers and adventures, was wonderful.

For some hours they travelled, and every one brought them nearer the place they sought. The sun had mounted high before they paused again to rest. On a fallen tree they sat, and talked of the joyful moment when they should reach home, and their wild adventures be ended.

Scarcely had they resumed their way, when Ralph paused, his quick eye having detected moving forms through the trees in advance. He gave a single glance, and then pointed them out to Nancy.

"See," he remarked, indicating them; "there come the men who suppose their sacred duty is to hunt me down and slay me. They have even gone so far as to organize themselves, with a view to scouring the forest until I am found."

"But they cannot harm you now," said Nancy, with some show of alarm.

"Certainly not, Nancy dear. But do you step behind that tree, while I advance a little, and you shall see the manner in which they greet me."

The maiden did as requested, hardly knowing how or why. Ralph then advanced several paces, and paused as he was noticed and eagerly pointed out by the leader of the party. Several of them at once set up a shout, and rushed toward the young man, who, to their surprise, did did not turn or flinch at their approach. Fearing some stratagem, they came on more cautiously, and were only withheld from firing by the hope of taking him alive.

Finally they had approached so near that half a dozen rifles bore upon him point-blank, and then the crowd pressed eagerly up. William Rufus, as ever, was foremost, and his manner, now that so decided a success had crowned his efforts, was jubilant in the extreme.

"Ha! my fine fellow, you won't try any more of your fine games upon us. We've got ye now in full daylight, and if anything is goin' tew interfar', we'll put a hunk o' lead threw yer karkiss. We've hed a pesky long hunt fer ye, right in the middle of the season, and lost a 'tarnal many good days' works. But, we's bound tew hev' ye, if we'd a' lost every day this summer. Such a confounded scapegrace as you wan't goin' loose, nohow, to stab people in the back in the night!"

"My good sir," said Ralph, somewhat sarcastically, "all your trouble has been for nothing. I never committed this deed of which you have seen fit to accuse me."

"That is your story for it; but it'll want one or two witnesses to prove it."

"I have the best witness in the world—the only one besides the murderer who saw the blow struck. She will tell you who is the guilty one."

"And who may this 'she' happen to be?" demanded Rufus, perhaps suspecting the truth.

Ralph did not reply in words, but turned and motioned

to Nancy, who had been an anxious witness of all that
had transpired. The maiden came forward quickly, for
she had feared some violence to her lover. As she gained
his side :—

"This is my witness !" he said proudly. "You cannot
ask for a better."

"Young woman, we want you to tell the truth about
this matter," said Rufus, who appeared somewhat crest-
fallen. "We want speshil jestice done, and the man that
killed yer father shall suffer for it, no matter who he is.
Now, don't be afeard to tell the truth all out; 'cause
we've spent our time jest to clear up this thing."

"I am ready to tell you all I know," replied Nancy,
with something of bitterness, as she thought of the in-
justice they had done to her lover. "But it seems to me
you would have shown more of the spirit of gentlemen
had you waited till reason and evidence condemned,
before you undertook to execute an innocent person.
Shame upon you—you especially, William Rufus, who
seem to have been a master-spirit of the mob !"

All but the person addressed slunk back, abashed by
the heroic maiden's words. He pressed forward, and in
the smoothest of tones, began :—

"You see, Nancy, we have no laws away here, and if
we had them, nobody, reelly, to put 'em in force. So we
hed a meetin' o' the folks, and banded ourselves for
muteral pertecshin—"

"Is this a specimen of your protection ?" she interrupted
him to inquire.

"Wal, never mind, Miss Andrews," he said, irritated
at the aspect affairs were taking, "we understand all o'
that. Now if you'll tell about that murder—"

"That I will do if will you give your attention, and

only interrupt me to ask pertinent questions.   I am not
in the habit of addressing a mob."

"Go ahead, miss," broke in a burly frontiersman,
"and if he don't keep mum, we'll shut off his breathin'-
pipes !"

All promised attention, and then Nancy related her
story :—

"On that fearful night I was sleeping soundly, as
usual, when I fancied one of the boards beside my bed
creaked.   I started up to look for the cause of this
singular noise, when, whom should I behold but a
stealthy Indian in my chamber !   I would have called
for assistance, but before I could do so his heavy hand
was placed over my mouth, effectually preventing any
outcry, and nearly smothering me.   'Now you dress,' he
said savagely, ' or me kill you.   Elk's Foot want you for
his bride.'"

Ralph gave a perceptible start as the Indian's name
was mentioned, but uttered no word.   When previously
relating her adventures, Nancy had not given the
Indian's name in its English dress.

" I was sorely frightened," the speaker went on, "but
dared not disobey, since he pointed to a knife and tomahawk in his belt, and threatened my life.   I did not
think he could leave the place, and was not so utterly
frightened as I should have been had I but known what
was before me.   I dressed hastily and when all my
clothes were secured, he led me down-stairs, still whisper-
ing threats of death if I made any noise.

"On reaching the floor, a second Indian sprung up,
and glided away to the bedroom where my father was
sleeping.   I should have attempted to cry out now,
regardless of my own fate, but the Indian who had me

in charge prevented my making any noise. I heard a scuffle, and presently saw the two figures struggling together. Soon my father's strength seemed to fail, and I saw the Indian deal him blow after blow with a knife, till he sunk to the floor. Then the murderer threw down the weapon, and ordered his tool (for the master-villain I found to be Elk's Foot himself) to take me out of the place, and with one or two warriors to take me home, and keep me there till he came.

"I was immediately hurried off, and knew neither rest nor sleep till I reached the Indian town. There I was treated kindly, and an Indian beauty, Sleeping Fawn by name, used every exertion to induce me to wed with her brother, who was heir to one-half the tribe in his own right. But I steadily refused, and finally succeeded in escaping. For two days and nights I wandered about in the forest, sometimes right and sometimes wrong, but managing to keep clear of the Indians. Finally, I fell in with Ralph, and after another captivity and escape, we were going back to demand reparation for the wrong you had done him."

"But about the knife," said Rufus, who was determined not to be convinced.

"Of course I do not know," she replied. "It does not matter. I saw the man that did the deed, and saw him throw the knife with which it was done in one corner. The man was Elk's Foot, but I know nothing of the weapon he used."

"You can swear to all this, I reckin?"

"If my word is not sufficient, take me before any person authorized to administer an oath, and I will swear to all I have stated."

At that moment, one of the men, who had been casting

120 THE DOOMED HUNTER.

anxious glances around while listening to the maiden's story, uttered a hurried exclamation, and pointed into the forest.

" By George !" he said, "the Indians are down on us, sure as fate !"

All looked in the direction in which he had pointed, and sure enough, within long rifle range, appeared a body of Indians, considerably outnumbering the whites. They were led on by Elk's Foot, who seemed foaming with rage, and ready for any desperate act. His followers came on at a full run, and it seemed their intention to take the whites wholly by surprise.

But the latter had come fully armed, and were prepared for any onset. Quickly unslinging rifles and crouching behind a large fallen tree and such standing ones as presented, the party were ready for the contest before the savages were fifty yards nearer.

" Take the gal and fall back out o' the way," said one of the men earnestly, addressing Ralph. " Ye hain't no gun, and ain't o' no 'count here."

" Nancy is quite as safe here if she will keep behind a tree," said Ralph, "and I shall not leave till I am forced to. Some of you may be wounded, in which case his gun must not lay idle."

" Good for you !" was the earnest return.

In a moment more the conflict was raging. The Indians advanced rapidly till the first volley from the whites laid three or four of their number upon the ground, when they took to trees, and opened a scattering fire. Both parties were now playing at the same game, but it was very soon apparent that the whites were having the best of it. The savages had but few guns, and these they could not use with the skill that characterised the whites. One after another fell killed or wounded, chiefly the former.

Presently a tall Indian burst from the cover on the right, and sprung across with rapid strides towards the left. He had nearly gained one of the larger trees, when a rifle cracked, and he plunged forward, falling in a kind of heap upon the earth.

Immediately the savages raised a despairing cry, and presently the survivors were seen hastening away by the most covered routes. The cause was certainly mysterious to the whites, but Ralph soon threw light upon it.

"That Indian, who fell yonder, is Elk's Foot, the murderer of Jehonikam Andrews, and several of your best citizens. He has fallen, and the balance of his band has fled. But he may not be dead yet. You can, perhaps, learn from his own lips the Indian's agency in that affair."

The impulsive men sprang from their place of conceal-ment, and to the spot where Elk's Foot had fallen. He was not dead, nor did he seem severely injured. The rifle ball had broken his leg, and that, in connexion with his wounded arm, rendered him quite helpless. He regarded the victorious whites with a fiendish expression, but preserved silence until questioned. Then he readily confessed the share he had taken in that brutal trans-action, and gloried in it, after the manner of his people.

"Look a-here," said the tall individual who had spoken once before, "here is the rope we brought out tew hang the murderer with, and I kalkilate we'd better use it now we've found the one!"

The rope was prepared quite as quickly as it had once been for Ralph, and this time there was no reprieve. The quivering form was strung up, and hung in the air.

For some moments the contortions were fearful. Then a tender-hearted executioner raised his rifle, and by a well-directed shot terminated the struggle. The soul of the base and cunning redskin had fled the earthly tenement for ever.

"See here, Ralph," said the same tall backwoodsman who had previously urged the execution of Elk's Foot, " I was wrong all the time—I want tew ax yer pardin for what I done ag'in ye? I sw'ar, I tho't 'twar' all right !"

" And so with me."

" And me."

Thus one and another urged, and readily the hunter forgave them all, shaking the hand of each as it was extended. Then a procession was formed, and with Ralph and Nancy in the centre they reached the little village of Forest Valley just at dark. Of course, every one was pleased at the return of Nancy, and thankful to find that their suspicions of Ralph's guilt had been unfounded. But for the dark cloud of sorrow which rested over their village, a merrymaking would have been the form in which to express their pleasure. Now, however, they gathered in little groups, and discussed the matter, vieing with each other in acts of kindness and attention to the sorrowing.

And now our story must end, much as all good stories should end. True love and honour were finally rewarded, and the silken cords of matrimony eventually bound Ralph and Nancy together in the holiest and dearest of earthly relations. That they lived happily we have abundant evidence from the records of the times.

LONDON : W. J. JOHNSON, PRINTER, 121, FLEET STREET

ROUTLEDGE'S SHILLING NOVELS.

By J. FENIMORE COOPER.

In fcp. 8vo, fancy covers, 1s. each.

THE PILOT.
THE PIONEERS.
THE DEERSLAYER.
LIONEL LINCOLN.
THE BRAVO.
THE TWO ADMIRALS.
THE WATERWITCH.
WYANDOTTE.
MILES WALLINGFORD
THE PRAIRIE.
THE HEATHCOTES.
PRECAUTION.
MARK'S REEF.
THE LAST OF THE MOHICANS.
THE SPY.
THE PATHFINDER.
THE RED ROVER.
THE HEIDENMAUER.
SATANSTOE.
AFLOAT AND ASHORE.
EVE EFFINGHAM.
THE HEADSMAN.
HOMEWARD BOUND.
THE SEA LIONS.
OAK OPENINGS.
NED MYERS.

GEORGE ROUTLEDGE & SONS, Broadway, Ludgate Hill.

JAMES GRANT'S NOVELS.

Price 2s. each, in Fancy Boards.

THE ROMANCE OF WAR; or, The Highlanders in Spain.

THE AIDE-DE-CAMP.

THE SCOTTISH CAVALIER.

BOTHWELL.

JANE SETON; or, The Queen's Advocate.

PHILIP ROLLO.

LEGENDS OF THE BLACK WATCH.

MARY OF LORRAINE.

OLIVER ELLIS; or, The Fusiliers.

LUCY ARDEN; or, Hollywood Hall.

FRANK HILTON; or, The Queen's Own.

THE YELLOW FRIGATE.

HARRY OGILVIE; or, The Black Dragoons.

ARTHUR BLANE.

LAURA EVERINGHAM; or, The Highlanders of Glenora.

THE CAPTAIN OF THE GUARD.

LETTY HYDE'S LOVERS.

CAVALIERS OF FORTUNE.

SECOND TO NONE.

THE CONSTABLE OF FRANCE.

The above in Cloth Gilt, 2s. 6d. each.

GEORGE ROUTLEDGE & SONS, Broadway, Ludgate Hill.

www.ingramcontent.com/pod-product-compliance
Lightning Source LLC
Chambersburg PA
CBHW032013010726
47493CB00007B/2387